curled in the bed of love

curled
in the bed
of love

stories by

catherine brady

THE UNIVERSITY

OF GEORGIA PRESS

ATHENS

AND LONDON

Paperback edition published in 2012 by

The University of Georgia Press

Athens, Georgia 30602

www.ugapress.org

© 2003 by Catherine Brady

All rights reserved

Designed by Mindy Basinger Hill

Set in Electra and MetaPlus by Bookcomp, Inc.

Printed digitally in the United States of America

The Library of Congress has cataloged the
hardcover edition of this book as follows:

Brady, Catherine, 1955–

Curled in the bed of love : stories / by Catherine Brady.

xii, 193 p. ; 21 cm. — (Flannery O'Connor Award
for Short Fiction)

ISBN 0-8203-2545-7 (hardcover : alk. paper)

1. Love stories, American. 2. San Francisco Bay Area
(Calif.)—Fiction. I. Title. II. Series.

PS3552.R2375 C87 2003

813'.54–dc21   2003006539

Paperback ISBN-13: 978-0-8203-4220-7

ISBN-10: 0-8203-4220-3

British Library Cataloging-in-Publication Data available

FOR ILSE KAHN

I dreamed that I died: that I felt the cold close to me;

and all that was left of my life was contained in your presence:

your mouth was the daylight and dark of my world,

your skin, the republic I shaped for myself with my kisses.

PABLO NERUDA, "NIGHT," XC

contents

Acknowledgments   xi

The Loss of Green   1

Comfort   19

Nothing to Hide   35

Honor among Thieves   54

Curled in the Bed of Love   73

Light, Air, Water   87

Side by Side   106

Thirteen Ways of Looking at a Blackbird   124

Roam the Wilderness   143

Written in Stone   162

Behold the Handmaid of the Lord   179

acknowledgments

The stories in this collection owe more than I can say to the editorial acumen and persistent faith of Steven Kahn, my first reader, my dearest friend. For their comments on individual stories, I am grateful to Linda Brady, Aaron Shurin, and Maureen Brady. Margaret Hansen, Patricia Hein, Mary Nisbet, and Tim Sheils made helpful suggestions along the way. Aaron Shurin, Deborah Lichtman, and Lewis Buzbee, my colleagues in the MFA in Writing Program at the University of San Francisco, have been extraordinarily generous in their support for my work. Last but not least, I want to thank David and Sarah Kahn, just because.

The following stories have appeared in the following magazines:

"Behold the Handmaid of the Lord," in *The Cimarron Review* (spring 2002)

"Comfort," in *Nua: Studies in Contemporary Irish Writing* (fall 2001)

"The Loss of Green," winner of the 2000 Brenda Ueland Prose Prize, in *Water-Stone* (fall 2000)

"Nothing to Hide," in *Other Voices* (fall 2000)

"Light, Air, Water," in *Natural Bridge* (fall 2000)

"Thirteen Ways of Looking at a Blackbird," in *The GSU Review* (spring 2000)

"Curled in the Bed of Love," winner of the 2001 *Zoetrope: All Story* Short Fiction Prize, in *The Cimarron Review* (spring 2003) curled in the bed of love

the loss of green

Every night, Sam makes Claire and Russell dance. He pushes the sofa and chairs against the wall, rolls up the rug, and puts one of the CDs he brought with him on the CD player. In the three weeks he has been staying with Claire and Russell, he has abolished the neatness by which they live their daily lives just as he's thrashed their habit of early evening hours. He filches more books from their shelves than he could possibly read at once, scatters books, maps, and unpartnered socks throughout the house, and marks his trail with plates and knives rimed by butter, bread crumbs, rinds of fruit. Claire is grateful that he works like a demon during the day, writing in the shed that Russell built for her on the bluff below the house, and just as grateful that at sunset he comes back up to the house to batter them with his careless, teeming presence.

Given Sam's hearty appetite for novelty, Claire is not surprised by his enthusiasm for ballroom dancing. And what Sam loves, he generously forces on others, so that Claire isn't certain whether she and Russell have been coaxed or bullied into learning to tango.

Sam makes Russell lean Claire backward, razzing Russell about looking into her eyes. "Never break eye contact, never. Come on, Russell. You are seducing her. Hold her like you mean it."

Russell laughs. Russell likes everything Sam dreams up for the evening, like a growing boy who enjoys whatever is put on his plate. When Russell pretends to lose hold of Claire, Claire clutches at his arms, and Sam shakes his head in disapproval.

Claire ends the lesson, as she does every night. She's still physically weak from her miscarriage three months ago, still finds herself suddenly exhausted by the effort to accommodate Sam's desire for fun.

Claire flops onto the cast-aside sofa and grabs the wine bottle that Sam has hogged while he ordered them around the room. He will be here for another month, finishing his book of nature essays. He wants to call it *Wild to the Bone.* He's managed to stay wild enough, never settling, never stooping to more than temporary work when he can't sell any freelance pieces, wangling his way onto naturalist junkets around the world, daisy-chaining together a string of women, none of whom has ever given him pause.

Claire and Russell sit together on the sofa, and Sam perches on its arm, jealously regarding the generous portions of wine they pour themselves.

"Claire, I wish you would wear a dress to dance class," Sam says. "Something sheer. Orange."

"And I wish you would wear fuzzy bunny slippers," she says.

Sam reaches over and draws his fingers through the thick black tuft of Claire's hair, shaped to frame her face and fan bluntly at the nape of her neck. "You could wear a flower behind your ear if you still had long hair."

Russell never seems to mind Sam's intimacies. Sam is the only one of Claire's former lovers who has remained a friend. That life, that wild life of Claire's before she met Russell, is over now, and Russell is the rock on which she hauled herself out, out of the chaotic sea of hard-drinking, hard-partying, heart-smashing, promiscuous years when she still believed that suffering was a kind of vocation.

Russell puts on a CD of Jacqueline du Pré playing Boccherini's cello concerto and turns out the lights so they can see the stars beyond the windows. Situated on a bluff at the tip of tongue-shaped Tomales Bay, the house faces the water, walled by windows that let in the night sky as gloriously as they let in the daylight view.

Sam grumbles. "Why do we have to have a show? Why can't we go outside and stumble around if we want stars?"

"Shut up and just take it in," Russell says good-naturedly. "You're the self-proclaimed Man of Nature."

"There is no nature with a capital N," Sam says. "That's a whitewash, that religious crap."

Claire's study, like the living room, faces the marshy flats where the land and the bay contend for dominance, fields of rich alluvial soil where dairy cows move slowly as silt, with Inverness Ridge to the west and the bay itself a crescent of blue foil at the horizon. She can't imagine feeling anything less than holy reverence for this place, the gift she mines in her thin books of poetry, and even the obscure destiny of her books seems of a piece with the humility awe engenders.

"Excuse me," Claire says, "but it sounds like you're the one preaching."

"It's always two against one around here," Sam says.

Russell yawns. "I need to get some sleep."

Sleep is hard to come by with Sam around. Tomorrow morning at six, Russell will roll out of bed and climb into the car, a cup of coffee in his hand, to drive two hours from Point Reyes Station into San Francisco, where he practices immigration law. He's negotiated a four-day work week, but it's still a lot of driving. Claire, who commutes only two evenings a week to the poetry workshops she teaches, takes on all the peripheral commutes for necessities that can't be found in their rural town.

When Claire inherited the house from her uncle, she and Russell never considered selling it, even though the house was built on the San Andreas Fault, the rift zone that records the efforts of the Pacific plate to move northwest and tug free of the North American plate, working for millions of years to take the coast of California, including the headlands to the west of them, with it. Geology is more metaphor than fact to Claire, and the secret strain in the earth beneath them makes her delight all the more in her solid house and lush garden. For Claire, moving here marked the completion of her reform. She thinks that for Russell, who was less sure, their move offered insurance against the risks she might incur in the city.

"Why don't you go on upstairs to bed?" Claire says to Russell. "I'll do the dishes." She looks pointedly at Sam. "Maybe I can get someone to help me."

"Leave them 'til morning," Sam says. "Give entropy a chance."

Claire gets up. If Sam is going to stay here for another month or so while he finishes his book, he'll have to earn his keep. "Let's go."

"Just when I was going to ask you to adopt me," Sam says.

Claire's eyes meet Russell's. It's so like Sam to trip carelessly on the wide and shallow root network of their recent loss. He sleeps in the guest room that would have been the nursery, and he has happily taken over the writing shed Russell built for Claire so she would have a separate space to work once the baby came. Claire has never used the shed. Someday, Russell promises. She has miscarried three times. A bout of endometriosis in her twenties, belatedly treated, has made it hard for her to get pregnant at all. At thirty-eight, she isn't sure she wants to keep trying.

In the kitchen, Sam hinders rather than helps. He blocks Claire's path from the sink to the butcher-block island so he can tell her about a camping trip in Yellowstone with his old girlfriend Andrea, boasting of their rowdy and constant sex in the tent.

"One day we came back from a hike, and the tent was torn up. It had to be the smell of sex that attracted the bear—we'd cached the food far away, like responsible ecotourists. I just wished we'd gotten back in time to see the grizzly at it. I've never laid eyes on one."

A little sparrow inside Claire pounces on this tempting morsel, a grizzly demolishing the flimsy temple of love, and gulps it down, guiltlessly driven by metabolic need. She's less quick to swallow Sam's declaration that Andrea broke his heart. More likely, Sam left Andrea, not brutally—he's a cowboy, not a conquistador—but in such a way that he could allow himself to feel wounded, regretful. That's how he left Claire, and quite a few women since. Claire couldn't let Sam go easily: she hunted him down at bars, to weep in his arms as he tried to lead her somewhere private; she spent sleepless nights smoking and drinking and scrawling bitter poems; she tore the poems into tiny pieces and mailed them to him.

"You have to cut your losses in bear territory," Sam says. "And I don't see why they shoot the bears when there's an attack. It's usually human carelessness, or stupidity, that provokes the attack. They ought to shoot the humans."

Sam is like a grizzly himself, looming and large and territorially rapacious. He doesn't even realize that he's backed her against the counter.

"I don't feel like sleeping, do you?" Sam says. "Let's go kill another bottle of wine and play some poker. Strip poker would be my preference, but I'll understand if you only want to play for pennies."

Claire hasn't wanted sex since the last miscarriage. Maybe her bottled-up instinct exudes a scent that provokes Sam, arouses his marauding desire. She has to push him to get him to step back from her.

Sam wants to hike around this end of Tomales Bay, and he doesn't want to get in the truck and drive to the trailhead in the state park.

Not when they can walk through the gate below the writing shed and take a path along the bluff. Claire explains to him again that they can't trespass on the dairy farmer's land.

"You never used to be so finicky." He tugs the rusted gate open and walks off.

Claire follows him. They are cheating anyway. They hardly ever shirk the discipline of their work days. Claire often feels she owes it to Russell, who is right now dutifully putting in a ten-hour day, to work strictly in his absence, to earn their three-day weekends in the garden or hiking in the abundant wilderness here.

She and Sam don't walk in silence for long. Sam is full of questions, sucking down whatever information Claire can provide about their surroundings. She explains that the summer gold of these California hills is not natural, but the consequence of over-grazing by cattle in the early days of European colonization. In its natural state this place would have remained green all year round. Claire regrets the loss of green as keenly as if she once knew it.

Claire doesn't mind Sam's questions, since she too is a de-vourer. She keeps notebooks full of notations on the color of ripening peaches, the drift of chameleon fog over the hills of the Inverness Ridge, the number and shape of the petals on a lily. She must take in a disproportionate excess of detail to feed the slender body of the poem that will eventually emerge, a compound of greedy pleasure and disappointment that the senses can't dam and hold the world in words.

They follow a track of trampled grass along the sloping hillside. Sam tells Claire of walking through golden fields of grass in a game preserve in Botswana, coming suddenly upon lions who held their ground because they must have had a fresh kill nearby, and pissing his pants with fear. Claire smiles. Sam must have his nature red in tooth and claw.

Barn swallows dart past them, tilting like paper airplanes on the breeze, flashing their russet bellies. The trail leads into a tightly packed thicket of bushes and trees, and Sam pushes branches aside and crouches to move in the compacted space. Following him, Claire ends up crawling on her hands and knees. When they come out, they are trapped by a creek, its muddy bank scalloped by the hooves of cows. Sam wants to wade through it, water up to his ankles, but Claire refuses. When they were lovers, Sam favored walks that required fording rivers, climbing steep, rocky slopes, leaving the trail and getting lost in the woods at dusk.

They return the way they've come, still at a military pace, with Sam eager to try every fork in the path. Claire often walks here with Russell, and they meander, not even aware of which path they choose. They talk very little about what they see—they need only touch one another or point—but a lot about Russell's work. Russell, who shrugs out of his suit jacket and into jeans as soon as he arrives home, is buried by the copious paperwork the INS requires, must share his clients' anxiety over their poor odds for victory, and he sheds the pressures of his work by spilling them here.

When Claire and Sam are again halted, this time by the farmer's fence, he holds barbed wire apart for her so she can follow him through. As they walk down toward the fingerlets of water where the bay and the streams that feed it first intermingle, they surprise a flock of seven white pelicans. The big birds lift into the air, unwieldy as laden bombers, their fight with gravity making Claire hold her breath.

The pelicans settle again in the water with timid fuss, like ungainly, plain girls invited to the ball after all—there's something so pleased and modest about their tucked heads. Claire asks Sam to stop and sit down to watch them. Overhead, a turkey vulture circles as it searches for carrion, its silhouette a gently sloping V, the feathers at its wing tips articulate as fingers.

"I never pictured you ending up in a place like this," Sam says. "You were such a city girl."

"Me? When we met, we were living in the country, remember?"

"A little college town in New England hardly qualifies as raw country."

Claire met Sam on a sidewalk, introduced by a woman in the graduate program Claire had just begun and Sam was just finishing. He was moving into a house down the street from Claire's, carrying a mountain bike over his shoulder and two disk-shaped weights in his fist. For Claire, it was disdain at first sight. A few days later, when she was passing his house on the way to campus, Sam startled her by coming around from the back and dragging her into his yard to watch a snake eating a frog. No words sealed this mutual seduction, only that fierce death they witnessed, the frog squirming and kicking as the snake's muscles forced it down the long tunnel of its digestive tract, the snake enduring that terror and panic in order to swallow it whole. Sam had given Claire a poem to write.

Claire looks up at the vulture still wheeling above them. "Where did you imagine me ending up?"

"I thought you'd stay in New York. In some little apartment crammed with African fetishes and Mexican pottery. I thought you'd run through men the way that I run through women."

"Been there, done that."

"You're like another person."

Russell introduced Claire to mornings in bed with the Sunday paper and coffee, to games played with flashlights under the covers when the power went out, to the names of flowers and their preferences for direct light or shade. He taught her that the world was a shell whose hinged mouth could be pried open to reveal a secret, smaller morsel of joy.

"I guess I am another person," Claire says. "I can't remember now why I liked the parties so much, and the men, from bad to worse, and swapping drugs with my friends. In case you didn't know, you should never mix downers and Prozac."

"Sounds like a Joni Mitchell song."

"Now you know why I don't talk about it."

The vulture keeps looping above them. There must be a dead mouse or a vole hidden in the grass, too close for the vulture to dare descending.

"Can I rent a kayak around here?" Sam says. "To go out on the ocean?"

"There's a place in town where you can rent one."

"I'd like to explore the coastline. You want to come?"

The coast is rocky, the surf perilous. Automatically, Claire rejects even the slightest physical risk, before she remembers that she's not pregnant anymore. A sonogram enabled her doctor to explain the mistake of nature that made her miscarry this time: the *corpus luteum*, an enlarged ovarian follicle that normally functions to produce the hormones needed to thicken the lining of the uterus and anchor the fetus, in Claire's body swelled like a cyst, filled with mysterious internal debris. No planning, no propitiation of the gods, could have prevented the random error.

"I might," Claire says. "It depends on whether you'd be willing to follow a few simple rules. Like staying out of the breakers. Like no tipping the kayak on purpose."

Sam squints at the vulture circling above them as if held in orbit by their presence. "I hate to have to tell you this, but one of us must be dead."

Claire flops back onto the stiff, brittle grasses, arms outstretched, and the vulture veers away at this sudden movement. Sam lazes beside her for a moment and then stands and peels off his shirt.

Claire sits up. "What are you doing?"

He shucks his pants. "I'm going swimming. I'm going to go say hello to those big white oafs out there in the water."

"Some militant environmentalist you are. Leave those birds alone."

"I've swum in a flock of brown pelicans before. They were feeding all around me. They're not fragile."

Cheeky thing. Those birds have survived on earth, nearly unchanged, for millions of years, and in comparison Sam and Claire are only dust motes in time's eye. But she knows better than to urge any modesty on Sam. Last weekend, when Sam, Russell, and Claire were driving out to the Point Reyes headlands, Claire steered around a dead skunk and then pulled over and walked back to drag it from the road with a stick so the vultures could feed in safety. Sam protested. "Don't interfere. We are not nature's housekeepers."

The birds scatter and regroup when Sam approaches the water. He wades in slowly, and Claire can imagine his feet sinking into the velvety silt. When he reaches deeper water, he dog-paddles silently, without a splash, and the pelicans slowly drift in his direction, close enough that he could reach out and stroke one of these abashed beauties. Slowly, he lifts one hand from the water and beckons Claire to join him.

She strips to her bra and underpants. Mud sucks at her toes until she too reaches deeper water. The birds have scattered again at her approach, and she and Sam have to wait for them to return. Claire has a moment when she fears the pelicans won't come back, fears her wishes are too extravagant to be granted. But soon the pelicans bob close enough that she can hear the clicking of their elongated beaks, see their yellow eyes, pools as mysterious and cool as amber.

Sam has a slaphappy grin on his face. He looks drunk. Claire should be grinning like that. But she's not. She has frayed the wiring of her nervous system so badly that the only electrical charge it can deliver is weak, erratic.

Though she doesn't trust Sam's reassurances, Claire goes along on the kayak trip anyway. They rent a kayak in town, load it into

Claire's truck, and drive along the shore of Tomales Bay. They put in at Heart's Desire Beach, argue briefly over who gets to sit in back and steer. Claire gives in and climbs into the front seat. They paddle clear of the shore, where at low tide the mudflats can strand a craft in a sticky goo that holds it in place but won't support your weight if you step out to reach shore.

Sam's questions peter out more quickly than usual, maybe because they are caught up in the rhythm of their work, maybe because the rhythm binds them to the intent purposefulness of this wild place. Turkey vultures cast off and circle on the air currents that curve around the flanks of Inverness Ridge, shorebirds poke methodically in the bay's muck, a kingfisher or two flits from its perch toward the water and back again to watch patiently. Claire and Sam are reduced to the simplest talk: *There! That flash of red in the trees—did you see that egret strike?* When Claire sits before her window at home, pad of paper in hand, she feels the same peace. All that is required of her is receptivity, the same kind of patience the kingfishers employ.

When they reach the rougher waters at the mouth of the bay, Claire and Sam pull out their oars and eat the lunch she has packed. Claire would turn back now, but Sam wants to leave the shelter of the bay and poke along the coast of the headlands.

"The surf is dangerous there," Claire reminds him.

"I know what I'm doing."

Again she gives in to him, reluctant to mar the accord of their bodies as they power the kayak through the water.

As soon as they round Tomales Bluff, the waves become choppy, and the wind pelts them with gusts of fog. It's harder now to work in rhythm with each other, the hollow kayak bucking on the waves. Claire shivers. They should have checked the weather prediction this morning. Russell consults the tide table when he and Claire are only walking out to the rocky coves where a fluke tide might trap trespassers. Sam says he'd like to go as far as Bird

Rock, which they can see in the distance, speckled with the dark bodies of cormorants. She turns to look at him. The waves punching at the boat, spraying his face and body, do not disturb him at all.

She doesn't want to count the number of times she and Sam drove back roads to find filthy, tiny bars where he would play pool and win no matter how he drank, teasing out the hostility of the locals in the same way he would flirt at parties until Claire betrayed annoyance, and then smile at her and deny intention. She doesn't want to remember enjoying that curiosity of his even when, their night finally at an end, they were followed out to Sam's car by the men who had been paying for his games all night.

Closer to Bird Rock, the surf is devious, the waves slapping at the kayak from a dozen directions, making it impossible for Sam to steer an even course. A wave smacks the bow directly, washing over Claire, so heavy and quick that she inhales salt water.

"I want to go back," she says.

"I think we can't." Sam shouts to be heard over the noise of the waves. "If we flip, lean in the direction of the roll, and we'll come back up."

She feels fear again, this companion of her wisdom, her painfully acquired care for her own survival.

Sam says, "We'll have to let the current take us past the rock. Once we get by, the water should be more predictable. We can head further out and circle back."

Now in the choppy rise and fall of the waves, the kayak clunks on its way down, smacks an air pocket before reentering the sea. Claire can no longer keep her paddle in the water; the torqued pounding of the waves would take it from her.

A wave smacks them broadside, and the kayak flips. Plunged into the cold, roiling water, Claire wants to fight free of the boat, free of the churning fists around her. But she leans, as Sam instructed, holding her breath until the kayak bobbles upright again to be slammed by another wave.

Sam praises Claire for hanging on to the paddle she didn't remember she had in her hands, urges her to stroke right, right, now left. She's so cold, her wet clothes so heavy and grasping against her skin. But Sam gets the kayak out past the breakers into deeper water, where they finally steer themselves toward safety.

Claire does not speak until they have rounded Tomales Point and returned to the predictable waters of the bay. "You knew what we were heading into. Your big ego. You just had to push your limits and see if you'd win the roll of the dice again."

"I didn't think it would be so rough. And it's not about my big ego. Didn't you feel it out there? How small your will is, how irrelevant? Come on, listen to what your body's telling you now. That gorgeous kick of adrenaline."

The fetid stink of the sea rises from Claire's clothes, heated to vapor by her body. If she weren't trapped in the kayak, she'd punch him. "There's nothing glorious about fear."

"Liar."

When they get back to the house after dropping off the rented kayak, its dented prow proof of the force they endured, Russell meets them in the entryway.

"Where were you?" he says. "You were supposed to be back hours ago. Dinner's ruined." He stops abruptly, takes in Claire's still wet hair, their soggy clothes. "What happened?"

"We took a roll in the kayak," Sam says.

"Sam had to have his thrill ride," Claire says.

"Next time you want to screw around, leave her home," Russell says.

For a moment, Claire thinks Russell might do something foolish, shove Sam's broad chest, take a swing at him.

But Russell is not by nature an angry man. He turns his attention to Claire.

"Better get out of those wet clothes. I don't want to risk you getting sick."

Russell commands Claire to sit on the bench in the entryway. While Sam stands beside her, fumbling with his shoes and stripping off his wet clothes, Russell unties the wet laces of Claire's shoes, fumbling with the waterlogged knot. When her shoes are off, he peels her wet socks from her feet. He holds an arm out to her. "You need a hot shower."

Claire declines his proffered arm. "I can manage on my own."

She takes a long shower, but the pounding hot water does not dispel the cold that has congealed in her body. The jeans and shirt she should put on are too heavy a burden, a reminder of the weight that soaked into her when they rolled in the ocean. She puts on a dress instead, not bothering with a bra, and stands shivering a moment before grabbing a bulky sweater and heading downstairs.

Russell has set a pot of tea on the coffee table, and Sam is digging into the plate of bread and cheese beside it. Russell offers Claire a cup. "This will do you good."

"I want a real drink," Claire says. But they don't keep hard liquor in the house.

"If I fix you a drink, will you forgive me?" Sam says.

"Don't count on it."

"Wait," Sam says. "Just wait."

He bangs around in the kitchen and brings back a loaded tray. On the coffee table he lays out everything he has collected for their drinking—cut limes, a bowl of salt, ice cubes, wide-rimmed glasses. He goes to his room and returns with a bottle of tequila that his father bought forty years ago, which Sam tells them he has been carrying around the world with him ever since his father died, the glass nearly opaque with age, the print on the label worn away by fingertips, the worm at the bottom hard as an acorn kernel.

Claire wets the rim of her glass with the lime, dips it in the bowl of salt until the rim glitters, then holds out her glass for Sam to fill with ice and tequila. Russell sticks with the tea. Until the drinks begin to take effect on Sam and Claire, they remain silent. Then Sam casts off on another of his pet peeves. He's been writing an essay on wildlife management, the transformation of wilderness into parks, a word he practically spits.

"Look at Yosemite," he says. "Paved trails, traffic jams, deer so tame you can walk right up to them, bears dependent on what they can scavenge from picnic coolers. Instead of limiting access, they're turning Yosemite into Disneyland."

"It would be undemocratic to keep people out," Russell says mildly. "People can learn to live within limits. They can be taught."

Russell's impulse is to help even when he can't accomplish anything by it. And not only in the persistent effort of his work, testing the rigid laws case by case. When they happen upon a wounded bird at the beach, he'll wrap it in his jacket and move it to the shelter of a rock above the tide line. Inevitably, when they come back along the beach, they'll find the bird, its throat torn by vultures.

"We don't have natural limits," Sam says. "Or we wouldn't have plundered our resources in the first place."

Claire downs her first glass as quickly as she can, spends more time preparing the next glass than she did drinking the first. Memory lurks in the taste of the tequila, in the way her hand closes around the wide-bowled glass. For years she has spoken of her relationship with Sam with amused tolerance, another example of her foolhardy waste of herself. Now she recalls drinking with him in a room lit only by dusk, Sam kneeling beside her, lifting the heavy wash of her hair, murmuring her name. She's frightened: that touch, the pealing of her name, more real than her numb body is to her now.

She reaches again for the tequila bottle. The liquor warms her. She shrugs out of her sweater while Russell doggedly argues with Sam, well able to hold his own, having earned his convictions by living up to them for twenty years.

"What every national park needs is a good bouncer," Sam says. "To turn back morons in RVs. To kick out the idiots who need TV sets in their campers."

"But you'd get to go where you want," Russell says. "No rules for you. Screw whatever happens as a result. Claire could have been hurt out there."

Claire looks at the glass in her hand. When was the last time she threw something? She places the glass carefully on the table and gets up and steps out the back door. She has not been this drunk in years. The stars swim above her, refuse to stay in place. She's astonished that they can disappoint her in this way, when she has spent hours watching the night sky, enough hours to learn how slowly the Big Dipper sinks toward the horizon, how it never dips far enough to spill over.

Russell comes out onto the deck after her, her sweater in his hand.

"Come on," he says. "We should go to bed."

Russell didn't rescue her. She chose him after she'd made up her own mind to change. She twirls away from him, letting the dress billow out around her. Sam, standing in the doorway, applauds.

When Russell moves toward her, Claire stumbles down the steps of the deck and dances in the garden, her arms out to the night. She is so warm. She plucks at the buttons of her dress, peels back the cloth to expose her skin to the cool air.

"Claire, Claire," Russell pleads.

She runs to escape him, feels as if she is floating over the grass. She remembers now how being drunk used to convince her of the grace of her body, how she never stumbled, never got sick, never banged into things. And something else comes to her belatedly: the awe that Sam promised her in the kayak and she denied. She feels wild with the knowledge of their dare, of the absolute moment when they were reeled under the water, when she did not have to ask herself, *Do I want to live?*

Russell looms closer, a blur in the dark, and she runs from him again. Twigs and stones prick her feet, but the sharp sensation doesn't hurt. She moves flawlessly and silently through the tangle of their garden and down to the bluff while Russell blunders noisily somewhere above her.

She crouches on the bluff just below the writing shed. The night swells around her like a luxurious blanket, muffling the movement of the body that appears suddenly beside her. Sam claps a hand over her mouth to still her cry of surprise and draws her quickly into the shed, tugging her to the floor. She can still hear Russell, moving noisily back toward the house.

Sam offers her a sip from the glass of tequila in his hand. Her senses, elongated by alcohol, discern the prism shape and sharp taste of each crystal of salt dissolving on her tongue.

"I've been wanting you to put on a dress," he says.

Smoothly, he slips her opened dress from her shoulders. The brush of his fingers against her skin shrinks her nipples to hard knots. He fishes the wedge of lime from his drink and runs it over her breasts, making her shiver. He leans over her to lick the taste from her.

It has been a long time since Claire felt desire. Her body feels full, as if the blood in her veins is holding still, pooling under Sam's touch.

He lowers his mouth to hers, his lips hard, his tongue seeking brutally in her mouth. His kisses, so unlike Russell's, demand a greedy response. As her hands roam over Sam's ribs, she shares with him astonishment at the strangeness of their contact—to have known each other's bodies so long ago is to have forgotten them.

But one hunger is kin to another and another, a span that knows no borders, and suddenly panic flutters in Claire's throat. She pushes up on her elbows, struggles to rise.

"I know," Sam says. "We shouldn't. But we can."

She raises her arm as a barrier. "No."

He rolls to the side, watches her tug at the disarray of her dress. "You'll come back. Another time."

She gets up and shuts the door, careful to let the latch click quietly, habit absurdly taking hold again.

She finds Russell sitting on the deck, waiting for her. She has a moment of hating him for his patient faithfulness. Then she sits beside him and curls her hand in his.

"If I could make it hurt you less," Russell says.

In the dark she can't tell where the land ends and the bay begins. Still she can faintly smell brine on the wind, discern the tree-tufted spine of the Inverness Ridge against the sky, imagine the waves pounding brutally at the unprotected shore beyond. This same glorious, erratic creation took their child, without intention, without malice, even though her body feels the blow as aimed.

Russell says, "We'll try again. We still have time."

The night loosens her, tugs her beyond the modest confines of reassurance. How still and solid darkness and the shapes it reconstitutes can seem, when below the surface the tectonic plates grind against each other with the accumulated force of sixty million years of yearning.

"I don't want to have to keep trying," Claire says, and now she can hear the low rumble of an ancient abyss, split, straining to open beneath her once again.

comfort

I've forgotten how long I told them I'd circle the block before coming back for them. Now I'm stuck behind a truck that's backing slowly into a driveway. I picture my customers standing on the corner looking bereft. Though they're more likely to be irritated, impatient, checking their watches to count off the minutes I've stolen from them, I prefer to imagine them as little lost lambs. Most people who rent a limo by the hour splurge only on a special occasion like a wedding or a prom night or a twenty-first birthday. They're usually so shy on finding themselves in the lap of luxury that I can't help wanting to give them their money's worth, hold doors open, provision them with champagne and fluted glasses, unfurl their umbrellas before they step out in the rain.

It's not like me to lose track of time. Probably I should make it a rule not to think about Linnie when I'm on the job. But we're at that point. Last night, my night off, she made me dinner at her apartment. Her best china, chicken stuffed with gooey cheese, lit candles on the table. After dinner we sat on the sofa to drink and talk, and she swarmed all over me, leaning against me when we kissed, running her hands up and down my chest, moving my hands down to her hips. It was nice. But when it didn't go any further than that, I could feel her tightening up, and she said, "Aren't you attracted to me?" And then I wasn't hard anymore. We've been going out for three months, and Linnie wants to have sex and I can't, and when she finds that out, there'll be no more cuddling on the sofa.

The customers do not look too angry when I pull up to the curb. Older people like Mr. and Mrs. Lesser tend to be more civil. I jump out of the car to open the door for them, apologizing, waving my arm vaguely and offering the one word, "traffic," as an excuse. I'm not sure how late I am, so I don't want to be too specific.

"We'd begun to wonder about you," Mr. L. says. Mrs. L. just smiles at me. With these older couples, the gentleman usually handles complaints.

"I know," I say gently.

"My wife left her coat in the car, and here she is, shaking like a leaf in this wind," Mr. L. says. "And paying for the privilege."

Mrs. L., her arms wrapped around her chest, truly does shake from cold. I reach into the car and get her jacket and put it over her shoulders. Still, she wraps her arms around herself, as if the cold has worked its way into her body and nothing will warm her now. I'm upset that I let her down. I want to wrap my arms around her, but she'd have a coronary if I did that. When I offer her my own jacket, I can tell by the way she looks at me that I've crossed the line.

I'm beginning to dread hurting these women almost as much as I dread confessing that I can't get it up. They think I'm such a catch—the women I end up with are slightly overweight like Linnie or gangly and bony, which makes them shy about taking off their clothes, which works to my advantage for a while—and they rush to blame themselves when I break up with them. I wish I had an excuse that would absolve them as well as me.

When I get back behind the wheel, I apologize again. "It's not like me to miss my cue," I say. "I'll make up to you for that lost time, I promise."

I hate it when people say the customer is always right, but what they really mean is the verbal equivalent of a shrug: let the idiots have their way. Mr. L. shells out all this money for a limousine, he expects something beyond transportation. The whole experience ought to reek of privilege: smooth driving, no cutting other drivers off or honking the horn, a stocked bar, helpful advice, some genuine concern when he has a particular need or wish.

"I'm putting on the heat," I say. "We'll warm you right up, Mrs. Lesser. You just tell me when the temperature's comfortable. And how did you like walking down the crookedest street in the world?"

I'd dropped them off so they could walk down the half-block or so where Lombard Street is cobbled and coiled like a snake. The line of cars waiting to drive down the few yards of the crookedest street in the world stretched for several blocks, and I figured, why should they have to wait?

"It wasn't what I thought it would be," Mrs. L. says.

"But now you can say you've done it," I say. With the tourists, you don't leave out any of the highlights, because they want to go home and say they did everything. So far this afternoon we've crossed the Golden Gate Bridge and come back, circled up to Twin Peaks, driven through the park, and toured downtown. Renting a limousine for a couple of hours is a good way to familiarize yourself with the city when you first arrive.

"That wind bites into you," Mrs. L. says. "You don't expect it this time of year."

I nod. "Summer in San Francisco is a rotten surprise."

I'm not your talkative type of driver. That kind of thing, where you're pressing your personal opinions on them and telling them your life story, is just oppressive to the customer, an intrusion. Of course I'll oblige if the customer initiates the conversation.

Some of the people I get, they talk my ear off. Maybe because the passengers don't have to look at my face—with my eyes on the road, I'm as anonymous as a priest behind the screen in the confessional—they pour out their hearts to me, or they want me to pour out mine. That's how I got together with Linnie. Right away, I liked her. She actually looked at me when she got in the limo. She asked me about the stack of books on the dashboard. I had James Joyce's *Dubliners* with me that day, and she'd read it too, and we laughed about how right he was about the Irish, all the mealymouthed *pleases* and *thank yous* and *I'm sorrys* slapped on over the grudges like a thin coat of paint. We talked about what part of Ireland our parents came from and the obvious things you have in common if you're Irish—a mother who's forever lighting a candle for you, wanting what you want but also always disappointed you haven't got it yet, and a father who hoards words like money but is plenty free with his fists. That's real Irish, all right. We sat parked in front of her apartment with the engine running, talked so long I ran out of gas.

As we head for Fisherman's Wharf, I give the Lessers a quick rundown of what they should do when they get there. Eat Dungeness crab from that stand on the sidewalk, watch for the seals on the west side of the wharf, stroll up to Ghirardelli Square to shop. I'm full of advice on where to find the best bargains.

I guess you get big ideas about yourself when you wear a uniform. I feel like a representative of something when I'm dressed for work: crisp white shirt pressed perfectly by the cleaners, the navy blue jacket and pants, shoes shined so you can see your reflection in them, and the cap, like a cop's cap, with gold braid above the rim. And I pay attention to personal hygiene, get a haircut every six weeks, trim my nails and buff them, keep an electric razor in the glove compartment so that when I work a long day I can still look fresh. A chauffeur's day starts at 6 A.M. when all the executives need a ride to the airport, and then you often get a slack time in the middle of the day. Business picks up again in the evening, and if you're driving a wedding party or even just a bunch of people who want to drink without worrying, you never know what time you'll make it home. Most nights I take the car home so I can clean it and be on time for the first charter the next morning.

My schedule has helped me out some with Linnie. I can tell her I just have a few hours free between customers or break off necking with her and claim I have to be up at five, and she understands. The problem is, those excuses can carry you only for so long. And I can't face trying again. I was twenty-one before I got close enough with a woman to have sex. Everything seemed to be working fine, but then when I entered her, I went soft. That poor girl—she worked on me, using her mouth, closing her hand over my penis and pumping it like a piston, till she was slick with sweat. The second time we were together, I managed to pull it off, but the third and fourth time she had to work so hard, and the more she had to work, the less aroused I got. So then you figure it's the woman. Till you've tried with five or six women, and it goes the same way with every one of them.

Worrying about why—if it was because I grew up Catholic, with Dad acting the tyrant and Mom playing the devout little handmaid, or if maybe I really preferred men—didn't matter much next to the fact that I couldn't deliver in bed. Failure piled up in the shape of a big brick wall. You have to wait for something bigger than you to come along and smash a thing like that. A miracle. So I'm killing time. For a couple of years now, during the midday slack period, I've been taking classes at the community college, and I do real well in my courses, but it's hard to finish them because I can never count on making it to class.

Mrs. L. asks me where she can buy some of the famous San Francisco sourdough to take home. "I'm sure you would know the best place."

She has real manners. When I recommend the Boudin Bakery, she thanks me with strict graciousness. I bet she has a spanking clean kitchen at home and makes Mr. L. mow the lawn weekly. I bet they go to a church with cushioned pews and no kneelers.

A crackling noise comes from Mr. L.'s corner, and I know he's studying the map. "There's a cable car turnaround right there by Ghirardelli Square," he says. "It looks like we could take the cable car back to the hotel afterward. Then we could let you go when you drop us off."

"Well, you could," I say. "But the lines are terrible. Too many tourists right there. I tell you what, though. I could pick you up when you're done and drop you off over on Bay Street. There's another cable car line there that not everyone knows about."

Mr. L. says, "We don't know that we'd find you when we wanted you, do we?"

Some people really want you to work for their forgiveness. And he probably assumes I'm trying to get another hour's fare out of them. I don't have another fare scheduled till six, and I really do want to make it up to him, erase the disappointment from his memory. "After that mix-up at Lombard Street, I'd like to treat you to an extra hour," I say.

"That's not necessary," he says.

He's embarrassed. The men usually are. When I get these businessmen in the car some mornings, offer them fresh orange juice or the newspaper, crisply folded, I have to insist on these little luxuries, and they'll take what I offer, if they take it, without a word. But the women, even the executives, are more open about wanting to be pampered. I'll glance in the rearview mirror and see them trying out the footrest or investigating the refrigerator just to see what they could have if they wanted it.

I try to come up with a way to get Mr. L. to see I really want to be generous, that I'm not just thinking of the tip. The other drivers think I'm a dope. Any little extras—drinks, food—the driver pays for out of his own pocket, and with the liquor especially, the hope is the customer will pay a dividend on your generosity when he leaves a tip. I stock the bar with Johnnie Walker Red; a lot of the other drivers just pour cheap scotch into a Johnnie Walker bottle. But I feel sorry for these guys, having to live all the time in falseness. That's the real misery to me. Then you're really a lackey.

"Mrs. Lesser's not gonna want to wait in that long line in this cold," I say. "And why should she when I'm right here?"

Once we can agree that we're doing this for Mrs. L., not him, Mr. L. goes along with the idea. I pull into a red zone so I can drop them off right smack at the foot of the wharf, because you're not restrained by the rules when you're riding in a limo, and then I make a big fuss of coming around to open the door, prolonging the moment when they can enjoy the envy of the pedestrians passing by us.

I pull away to find a place where I can park on the street for an hour. Parking is a nightmare in San Francisco, and you get so you know every little side street where there's a chance of finding a spot, just like you know the location of all the public restrooms. I look for parking near the housing projects, because the tourists take one look at the cinder-block buildings with rusted metal grilles over the windows and decide to fork over ten bucks for a parking garage. I pull into a spot and crack the window for some fresh air before turning off the engine. I might get a kid or two coming up to touch the car or peer in the windows, but as long as I stay with the car, I don't generally have to worry about any damage to the vehicle. The quiet on these empty streets is eerie, like the few stunted trees here, shaped like some scrawny struggle that's gone still, been frozen to silence.

I sort through the books on the dashboard, trying to see what I feel like. I usually keep half a dozen books with me, because if you're waiting for a customer who might return any minute, you can't concentrate on a heavyweight like George Eliot, and you need a mystery or a biography that you can pick up and put down constantly. When I know I have time, like I do now, I can dig into something solid, unless I'm just too tired to make the effort. I pick out a book of stories by Flannery O'Connor, which I am not having too much fun with, but which I feel I ought to finish, for the sake of my education.

This Flannery O'Connor is some kind of Catholic all right, and I suspect the brutal way she goes about her business stems from that Irish last name of hers—she and my dad would get along just fine. She makes fun of her characters the whole way through the story, and then she pounds them with something terrible, a mass murderer on the loose, a little boy who hangs himself. The father of this little boy is kind of an ass, a right-thinking liberal who wants to adopt a poor black kid but won't let his own child believe his dead mommy is in heaven. The guy just doesn't deserve what happens to him. I'd love a chance to ask old Flannery why she took it so to heart, the mean idea that salvation should cost too much, the eye of the needle and all that.

I get celebrity authors in the limo sometimes, and if they're chatty, I'll ask them that kind of stuff. They would shine me on if I mouthed pablum about how nice their books were, but they're surprised when I ask specific questions that show I've read the book. Like everyone else, they prefer to assume you're invisible. I'm not the only driver who's had customers get hot and heavy in the back, even though I might be the only driver who's doubly tormented by having to pretend I can't see it or hear it.

Sometimes the authors get over the initial shock. This one guy who wrote a book on the psychology of shopping gave me a whole song and dance about how Americans are finally working free of their Puritan roots and getting up the courage to be hedonistic. Shopping's a reward, an intimate pleasure, and the customer can't feel intimate if the store is too crowded or the merchandise is placed too close to where there's a lot of traffic. Women in particular, he told me, won't buy if they're worried about people bumping into them from behind. I understand that, I guess. The most luxurious thing about a limo is the stillness, the way you can seal yourself off from the rest of the world with the push of a button, settle into a cozy cave with carpeting that runs up the door so that you won't hear the soles of your own shoes scrape against anything.

When I told Linnie about this guy, who gets paid to videotape customers in a department store and analyze their behavior, she laughed. She claims all marketing research is hogwash, even though she herself fits this guy's profile to a T, buys in boutiques because she's embarrassed to pick through racks of clothes in department stores. Then she'll correct herself, say no, it isn't hogwash—"they" work on us every minute to transform all our wants into whims that only their products can satisfy. When she works for a marketing firm herself.

I'm never too sure about Linnie's job description—whether she's a glorified secretary or has really worked her way up into management. One minute she's showing off about her expense account—we'd never have met if her company wasn't a client of the limo service—and the next she's plotting ways to punish the executives for expecting their administrative assistants to work the same long hours they do for a fraction of the pay. I love her for that, for how she keeps bumping into herself coming and going, for how her own vehemence bangs smack into her confusion about what she really wants. She's going to get so tangled up in deciding whether I'm a jerk for breaking up with her or whether it's her fault for being too plump or too apologetic about her ample self, too assertive or too hesitant, too much woman or not enough. I'd tell her I had some neurological disease and it wouldn't be fair to expect her to sign on for that, except then Linnie would probably rise to the challenge.

I look up from my book when I hear the yelling. Surfacing from the book to reality is like stepping out of a dark room into the light, and I'm blinded, can't see them at first, though I can hear them. They're standing on the sidewalk just a couple dozen yards from me, a woman and a man circling each other, shoulders squared, screaming the usual fuckingbitchbastard at each other. They're from the projects: in the same way the scraggly trees here shout poverty, their clothes shout the tiredness and wear and tear and ill fit of a hard life.

For a few moments the man and woman are bound to each other, connected by a taut cord of tension, she moving to the left when he moves to the right, keeping exactly the same distance between them. Then he lunges for her, his fist slamming into her shoulder. She trips over the curb and tumbles into the street, rolling like a cat as soon as she hits the ground, preternaturally aware of just where his foot will come out to kick her, foiling him. Then she's up, shoulders hunched, circling him again, both of them panting, chests heaving with pent-up rage.

I bang on the window, but they don't even register the noise. I turn the key in the ignition so I can put down the automatic window and holler at him. If that doesn't scare him off, I can get the dispatcher on the radio and have her dial 911.

I yell once I get the window open—I don't even know what words come out of my mouth—and she's distracted by the sound just long enough for him to take advantage and slam her in the chest with his thick forearm. Her knees buckle, but she hits him back, glancing her fist off his jaw, almost losing her balance. Her stringy shoelaces are undone, and it seems like the cruelest thing that this handicap should be added to the disadvantage of her smaller weight and size.

Words tumble from my mouth, and now I know what they are. "Stop! Stop it!"

It's his turn to flick his antennae in the direction of another possible threat.

He gives her just enough time to crouch, grab something from the pavement, and smack it against the curb. When she lifts her hand, I see she holds a broken beer bottle by the neck, its circumference transformed into a curved blade.

I'm yelling, fumbling for the goddamn radio mike and dropping it beneath the seat. I shout at her to run, but now he leads the wary dance, afraid to turn from her, afraid not to mirror her every movement. She slashes, and he shapes himself into an S-curve as he jumps back from her. They're close enough to the limo that I can hear the raggedy caw of their heavy breathing.

Her determination to cut him makes her careless. She swings wildly, and he takes advantage of her momentum to smash her down onto the pavement again. She slashes at him even as she struggles to her feet.

I'm screaming now. I open the door and get out of the car, wishing I kept a baseball bat under the seat, something I could use on him. He turns in my direction, and she tackles him, knocking him aside so she can come straight at me.

She charges past me to fumble at the latch on the back door, and I feel this stupid reflexive shame that I didn't get the door for her. She scrambles into the backseat and slams the door behind her, and then she screams at me. "Go! Go!"

I fold myself into the car and slam the door and thank God I have the engine running. The guy charges at the car, pounding on the smoked glass of the window, and for a moment I imagine that his fierce assault makes the car shudder and jerk as I try to maneuver it. But it's me, my fear, my suddenly slippery hands that prolong the agonizing seconds before I've steered out of the parking spot and can step on the gas. He slips from the car and falls back onto his butt, and she lets out a short gust of air, almost a laugh.

Out of habit, I slow gradually for the stop sign at the corner and accelerate gently through the intersection. I feel remote from the calm practice of my body, and I can't tell the difference between the wretched sound coming from her and the rattling in my own throat.

I have to struggle to speak. "There's a radio mike somewhere back there on the floor. See if you can find it, and I'll get the dispatcher to call 911."

She curls into a ball on the backseat, arms wrapped around her chest, and goes on struggling for air. I try to dig for the radio mike on the floor, but I can't do that and drive at the same time. I pull over so I can search properly.

"No," she pants. "Don't call the police." She sits upright. "Don't do that."

"You can have him arrested."

She laughs, but it must hurt, because she stops abruptly. "Unh-huh. Now you gonna pop out the phone number of some women's shelter, I know that."

"I'll be your witness that he attacked you," I promise.

"I can believe that. You show up out of nowhere to fetch me in a limousine. I can believe anything."

"At least let me drive you to an emergency room." I know this city like the back of my hand, but I have no idea where the nearest hospital is.

She crawls forward jerkily, as if the car is still moving, and leans over the front seat to look into the rearview mirror. We both look at her reflected face. She must have hit the curb face first when she fell. Already her right cheek is swelling, closing up her eye, and her lip is split, seamed by a dark line of blood.

"What I'm supposed to do in some emergency room," she says. "Sit holding a towel to my face till they get around to me. They find out you got no insurance, they tell you you don't need no X ray anyway."

"I'll come in with you," I tell her. "I'll make them look after you."

She leans her forehead on the back of the seat, and by the way her shoulders shake, I think she's crying. But she's laughing. She looks up at me and grins, which must cost her a lot with that lip. "Who you think you are?" she says. "Fucking Mother Teresa."

This time I turn around to face her instead of meeting her eyes in the rearview mirror. With the swelling it's hard to tell what sort of face she really has. Nice eyes, brows drawn sharp and clean above them. A line grooves her cheek on the side of her face that isn't swollen, the kind you get from smiling a lot, or from bitterness. Her shellacked hair is pulled back from her face in a pom-pom of a ponytail. And I can smell her. A body's actual smells are usually banished in here—the customers sit too far back, and I douse myself with aftershave and men's cologne. She just smells like skin, warm skin that would be fragrant if not for the slick overlay of sweat, fear. She still has the broken bottle in her fist. I remember how expertly she wielded it, pursuing the fight when she could have run.

She looks where I am looking. "You scared?" She pretends she's not interested in watching my face for a reaction. But I'm too familiar with this kind of pleasure to mistake it for indifference. One too many times I've understood that for the people screwing in the backseat or snorting coke from a compact mirror, I'm necessary to the fun, present yet as invisible as Jesus H. Christ.

She sets the bottle down carefully on the carpeted floor where it will make no sound if it rolls, then looks back at the rearview mirror.

"I got to take care of my face," she says.

She inches back along the carpet, eases herself slowly and painfully onto the backseat, and fishes around in the mini-fridge. She pulls out a bottle of Evian water and holds it to her cheek, closing her eyes and sighing with pleasure.

"What do you want me to do?" I ask her.

Her eyes flicker open, then shut again. "That motherfucker got a car. Whyn't you drive me out this place? That's what you do, drive, so do it."

"Where?"

"Whyn't you just drive me—I don't know, all around."

"I'm going to stop somewhere and get some ice to put on that eye." I pull away from the curb. "Are you going to tell me your name?"

She takes her time deciding. "Mary."

Her name's not Mary. "My name's Pat."

She leans back, the bottle pressed to her cheek. "How you doing, Pat?"

"If you're hungry, there are snacks in the fridge."

I have to find a McDonald's or a 7-Eleven where I can get ice. At least I've driven to those places before. With prom parties or people out drinking. When I next look in the mirror, she's pouring scotch into a glass. She has to wince to sip it with that cracked lip, but she works at it steadily.

"What do people pay for this?" she says.

"Drinks are compliments of the driver."

"No. I mean, what they pay to ride in a limousine?"

"It depends. About fifty dollars for the first hour, less after that."

"And what for?" I think at first that she wants information from me, but she goes on talking. "I bet most of them can't afford it. But they so almighty in love with money they want to look fat even if it's only for a few hours. I bet they work you too, don't they? Fetch me this and fetch me that. Gotta squeeze all the privilege they can from their dollar. That's the only rights people got in this country. The 'I'm paying for it' rights." She meets my eyes in the mirror. "Stop looking at me like I'm a talking monkey. Just 'cause you folks can't see me don't mean I can't see you."

I'm not thinking what she thinks I'm thinking, but trying to prove it would amount to trying to prove I'm not a racist. Like that guy in Flannery O'Connor's story. I'm thinking that she talks like Linnie when Linnie's on the rampage, cursing out the bosses of this world for their subtle, tricky ways. Even the expression on her face right now makes me think of Linnie, who's so soft underneath it all, whose face can collapse into such tiredness.

"I don't know," I say. "Everybody wants a little comfort if they can have it."

"Yeah, right."

I pull into the parking lot of a McDonald's, and Mary asks me to get her french fries while we're here. When I get out of the car, the ground feels like a sea beneath me, roiling waves. That's how I know I'm still scared.

When I return and present Mary with the greasy bag and a paper cup of ice, she laughs. "Now I'm seeing why folks like this all right."

I could sit back there with her, but I have never sat in the back of the car, not even when I didn't have a customer. So I sit in front with the door open, watching her. She eats with slow, patient refinement, holding one french fry at a time between two fingers, dipping the fry into her scotch, and then gingerly taking it between her swollen lips.

She wipes grease from her fingers onto the leather seat, and worrying about the stain reminds me that I've forgotten the Lessers for the second time today.

"I gotta get back to work," I say. "I stranded a couple of tourists at Ghirardelli Square."

"I can get out here," she says. "I guess I oughta thank you."

"I can drop you at the police station."

"Whyn't you just wave your magic wand and make my problems disappear?"

The limp french fry flutters in her trembling hand. Her face is closed, as if to protect what I'll never see, a stale-smelling kitchen, maybe a kid crying in another room, that man rubbing her sore feet at the end of the day, that man's fury or hers flaring to life like a struck match, all the hard practice they've had passing along pain to a final resting place in each other's real flesh.

"What else am I going to do with you?" I say. "Drop you back at his door so you can take another crack at each other?"

"Get me some ketchup," she says. She rubs at the side of her face that isn't swollen, deepening the crease in her cheek till it branches like a crack in dry earth.

"Please," she says. "Then I won't bother you no more."

I never said she was bothering me. I get out to fetch the ketchup, and when I come back to the car, the back door is open and Mary has gone. She's left the broken bottle behind, staked its sharp edges into the plump leather of the backseat. When I pull the bottle out, a semicircle of leather peels up in its wake, a tiny mouth spitting fluffy bits of stuffing.

She shouldn't have taken off on me. I *did* rescue her. That blazing moment when she jumped into the car should have claimed us both. She's cheated me of the chance to see her through to safety, or at least relief. I get the Dust Buster and my housekeeping kit from the trunk so I can clean up after her. Worse than being late again for the Lessers would be inviting them into a car still reeking of McDonald's, and I've chauffeured enough kids on prom night to be prepared for any emergency.

I squirt orange-scented air freshener, use the Dust Buster, and then tape up the torn seat. Running my hands over the leather, I can still feel tiny grains of salt from her french fries, like the briny remnants of some ancient sea, the crystals of what should have been the cleansing wash of her tears.

It's my fault. I had this one real chance, and I let her down.

I wonder if the Lessers are still waiting hopefully for me to return. I sit down for just a minute. Sinking into the overstuffed seat feels like settling onto the ample lap of a giant. I pull the door shut, and I'm truly cocooned in the lush silence of the car. I think I'll tell Linnie the truth after all. Maybe she'll be OK with it. I stroke the leather seat. Smooth as warm skin. Skin so thin a sheath between us.

nothing to hide

Hannah sings to herself without even knowing she's doing it, sings in the bathtub, sings when she comes home from school and dumps her backpack on the floor, sings now as she loads the dinner dishes into the dishwasher. Sometimes she makes up the words as she goes along; other times she sings fragments of familiar songs slapped together haphazardly. In the faint wash of that trilling sound, I tug the clothes from the dryer in the basement. Any moment now, when her father brings her older brother home from his friend's house, she'll stop singing, shy of witnesses.

Once upon a time I would have taken advantage of Jay's ten-minute absence to drink down here by the washing machine, slugging down wine so fast that it would congeal in my belly to emanate heat like fuel. Even after two years, when these would-have-been opportunities arise, I feel unbalanced, lacking the counterweight of that guilty haste and deceitfulness, that snatched triumph.

I come up the stairs with the laundry basket in my arms to stand in the kitchen doorway and admire my daughter, who is racking dishes with the tiniest, most delicate hands. At ten she's still so small she has to stand on tiptoe to reach into the sink.

"Oh, I do, I do so want to dance with you," she sings to the plates.

"You know what I love about you?" I say.

She gives me a sly look. "Everything?"

The trouble with our kids is that they've become jaded. *Love* is a word that gets a workout in this house, a word that's spawned a host of pseudonyms and endearments to catch the overflow. Hannah has so many names by now I can't remember them all or even their etymology—Peewee Jones, Miss Miss, Princess of the World, Mistress Mouse. Nathan isn't far behind—Little Guy, Baby Boy, T.T., Cuddlemenschen.

I say, "The way you go around singing all the time."

"I think it's dorky. I've been trying to make myself stop."

"I like it," I say. "It's like living with happiness in the house."

With her dainty hands, she bangs a plate into the dishwasher hard enough to make me wince. "Oh yeah!" she sings. "I rule!"

The one place you don't have to be furtive about sneaking out for a cigarette is an AA meeting. At every meeting in the church basement there has to be a vat of coffee, regularly scheduled breaks for the smokers—necessary tokens of nostalgia for our drinking days, the habit of wanting. Roberta and I huddle together on the church steps, the only die-hards willing to brave the cold for the sake of having a second cigarette.

Roberta shivers. "I wish I wasn't so goddamn compulsive."

"Do you want my coat?" I offer. Like my children, I'm more apt to go out underdressed for the weather than not, determined to deny that it's cold, like any good, self-respecting San Franciscan.

"That's your compulsion," Roberta says. "Have you ever wondered why you volunteer for everything? Why you're always the one who gives other people a ride home?"

I still have a driver's license, unlike a lot of the others. So it seems as if I have to say yes, even to Walter, when I don't like him.

He's been a recovering alcoholic for a while, but he's only been in our group for a month. He starts arguments at the meetings. In the car on the way home, he's loud, he fidgets, and if he's sitting in front, he reaches over and leans on the horn whenever he decides another driver deserves it. He yells "fuck you" out the window, which is always open to clear the smoke from everyone's cigarettes.

"Nobody else brings cookies to every meeting," Roberta says. "Homemade, at that. You don't have to please your mother anymore, Maizie."

Everyone here knows everyone else's secrets and taps into them at will to discover an ambiguous motive for the simplest gesture.

"That was never possible anyway," I say. There's no need for explanation—Roberta's my sponsor, knows the whole pathetic story. Which isn't much anyway. My mother struggled to raise two kids on what she made packaging chocolates at the See's candy factory with a vengeful fervor aimed at the husband who'd died on her, the managers at the factory, and her only daughter, who could never do enough to make up for any of it.

Roberta complains softly about her own mother. Her mother didn't talk. Not in sentences, only in clipped commands, one-word judgments—slut, bitch, ingrate. "When I had my son, I was eighteen, completely on my own, and she came to see me. She looked into the crib at the baby sleeping there and all she said was, 'bastard.'"

Tears well in Roberta's eyes. "This is silly. I don't know why I get like this."

But she cries on, and I cry with her. Often when we are out here alone, we cry together. I always think to myself, *get it out, get it out,* cheering myself on in the sob fest. When I don't even know what *it* is. I've got no reason to be unhappy: I have a good husband, two beautiful children who seem remarkably undamaged by my addiction, a nice house. About the only thing I suffer from is excess volunteerism: at the high school where I teach English, I'm always saying yes to the department chair when she needs someone to organize a conference, counsel problem students, join committees. I juggle my daily teaching schedule so I can race to pick up the kids from school at three, and I work nights after they're in bed.

The only unhappiness I can claim—my beaten-down mother who maybe had a right to her bitterness—is meager by AA standards and little more than a murky fog to me. I've been blessed by forgetfulness, can't remember much of my childhood at all. An inherited trait, maybe, like the alcoholism I share with my grandfather, the random accident of genetic predisposition. I barely qualify as a drunk—I was always careful, only drank after dark, never drove when I was high. I don't have a single story that might hold its own, even momentarily, in my fellow members' "can you top this?" exchange of past crimes, of childhood sorrows that are the firm, succulent roots of all their sinning and redemption.

Here is the thing about loving a man who stumbles when it comes to words. Jay has an astonishing facility at speaking through his body, through his eloquent hands. When I curl up against him after we make love, he strokes my back, and my nerves tingle under his fingers, emit pulses that chase his hand as he repeats a delicate trace-work on my skin, the echo of the satisfaction of our lovemaking. Jay's dyslexia might be what makes him so good at what he does for a living, just as it makes him so good with me. As a programmer he translates words and functions into binary operations, simple yes/no questions that branch out to the next, neat yes/no. As a lover he uses his careful hands to perform a similar feat, to elicit responses that trigger a chain reaction of yes.

Nothing's so nice as our sleepy postcoital talk about the kids, the thriving product of our love. We trade stories of their day the way that other lovers might trade bites of some delicacy to romance one another. I worry about Nathan being bored in school, and Jay simplifies things for me by dancing his hand along my spine and saying that he was bored in school too, and it's only a normal part of childhood.

I slip reluctantly from beneath his touch. "I have to go finish grading papers."

It's our usual routine for Jay to fall easily into sleep and for me to get up and squeeze in a few hours of work before coming back to bed. And it's Jay's usual response to wish that I wouldn't take on so much. I don't have to work full-time *and* be the mother who organizes phone trees and bakes for all the class parties. He needs so few words to tell me who I am.

"And then you top it off by making it to three AA meetings a week," he says. "Can't you taper off now?"

Jay will never know how much I used to drink, still thinks I volunteered even for the daunting task of being an addict. Without exactly putting it into words, he's let me know that he thinks I drank when the kids were little because I needed an outlet. I was an ambitious person, with nothing to do but take the kids to the park and make spaceships out of paper plates. I shouldn't have stayed home with them full-time. But I wanted to stay home with them. I don't regret a minute of the seven years I was a full-time mommy. I can't offer a better reason than his for why I drank then, when I was so happy with the kids, when taking them to the pediatrician for a checkup was a big event, a thrilling chance to show them off like two perfect jewels.

"You know I have to go," I say. "Besides, a lot of people count on me for a ride."

Jay laughs. "You're always so ready to feel guilty."

Guilty is one box among many, clearly labeled, conceivably avoidable if only one can answer *no* on the previous step. Jay likes to tease me about my Catholic guilt, cull it from the bundle of emotions I call my own. But even my name is a contraction of the

Irish Mary Elizabeth that leaves nothing out, only collapses the catholicity of my being so that it is more dense.

Roberta and I are crying again when the door to the church bangs open and Walter steps out. "Can I bum a smoke?"

Everyone else more or less grants us the right to this snatched privacy, but not Walter. He steps up too close to Roberta, as if to intimidate her into giving him a cigarette, oblivious to the tears streaming down her face.

Roberta brushes her open hands across her cheeks to smear tears, and then she fishes in her purse for a cigarette and a lighter. "You always bum."

Walter holds Roberta's wrist steady while he lights his cigarette from the lighter in her hand. When he straightens up, he exhales noisily. "How can you grudge me?"

He can't stand still. He shifts his weight from one foot to the other, moves down a step, then back up. Walter looks like everything that made me afraid to sign up for AA. His dirty hair is pulled back from his face in a careless ponytail, his shirttail hangs out, his face has *wreckage* written all over it. Our AA group doesn't have exactly the same composition as the mother's play group I used to belong to, but it's close. Just about everyone but Walter seems to be trying to lead a nice middle-class life. And Walter won't let any of the rest of us forget it, makes a point of coming to meetings in his work clothes—the grease-spotted shirt with the Chevron logo on a patch sewn over the pocket. He thinks he's the only working-class slob who ever walked the planet and enjoys telling the rest of us how coddled we are.

"Listen, Maizie," Walter says. "Can I have a ride home?"

"Sure," I say. "The more the merrier."

" 'Sure,' " he mimics in saccharine tones. "When are you going to drop this Girl Scout persona?"

"Tell him to take the bus," Roberta says.

Walter looms toward me, and it's all I can do not to step back from the assault. But he thumbs a tear from my cheek with astonishing gentleness. "Look at her," he says. "She's so precious, she cries little diamonds."

To get Nathan to stop reading so we can turn out the lights, Jay has to pull the paperback from his hands, and then he must take the book out to the living room so Nathan won't get up to read on the sly after we leave him.

While I smooth the covers and toss extra pillows from the bed, Nathan talks to me. He always wants to talk when we are about to say good night. He tells me that he's already memorized five prayers for his bar mitzvah. Even the morning prayer.

"I bet Dad doesn't even know that prayer," Nathan says.

Jay had a fairly secular Jewish childhood and probably knows very little more than I do about Jewish tradition. It was Hannah, with her religious little heart, who wanted to join a temple, and then I thought it wouldn't hurt Nathan, Mr. Fact and Reason, to nurture that side of himself. There's so much I love about Jewish tradition, starting with Jay and his family, their exuberant Passover dinners, and it's never crossed my mind to raise the kids Catholic, since my own religious upbringing has an aura of punishment to it, my mother pinching me in the pew for fidgeting, the audible hiss of someone's voice in the confessional, an insinuating, frightening sound.

"You know what the morning prayer is for?" Nathan says as I lean toward him to kiss him good night.

I straighten up. "No. What's it for?"

"They believed that when you went to sleep, your soul went away at night. So when you woke up in the morning, the first thing you had to do was thank God for your soul coming back."

I smile at his "*they* believed." The tiny mustard seed of faith is hardly sprouting in my son, but in me it finds tilled ground.

"That's beautiful," I say. I lean down again, hoping to finish the conversation with a kiss and a hug.

"You stink," he says when I release him. "You've been smoking."

I can't deny it. Caught again. He's old enough to have been drilled at school in the horrors of smoking. I don't smoke in the house. I go out in the backyard to have a cigarette, just as I go out on the steps with Roberta at meetings, so I won't poison the kids, so I can hide it from them. Still my son can smell it on me.

After the meeting ends, Walter begs a ride from me again and starts in on my other passengers as soon as I pull away from the curb. Walter has elected himself to be the man who keeps us honest, just as he's assumed the job of dictating my route when I deliver passengers, always working it out so that I bring him home last. I can feel the three people in the backseat holding themselves stiffly as if that will defend them from the ricocheting torment of his voice.

"You're all such gluttons for punishment," Walter says. "Can't get enough of it. Because you're hoping for the one punishment that will be enough, finally, to let you off the hook. Me too. I love it when my son throws the past at me. I deserve it."

After I drop off my next-to-last passenger, I'm scared that Walter's *you* will condense to a vindictive singular. I'm waiting to hear him accuse me of all kinds of things for the rest of the ride, but he doesn't. Instead he asks if we can't go by my house on the way to his place. He's just curious, he says. It's on the way, isn't it?

Maybe I have to offer him this in exchange for his silence. I turn up my own street, feel the car's engine strain on the hill, then slow down before my house.

I point it out to him. An Edwardian in a row of Edwardians that face the street, packed tightly together with tiny, carefully plotted flower beds on their shallow front lawns, their steep second-story roofs vaulting each of the upstairs bedrooms.

He puts a hand on my arm. "Stop," he says.

I stop. We look at the house, the pearly moonlike glow of light through the window shades that have been pulled down at all the windows.

"I should have known," Walter says. "Of course you live on a postcard street."

"Why do you have to make that sound like a crime?"

"Well, it's not a crime, is it?" he says.

We watch as a shadow drifts across the upstairs window. I'm proud of recognizing Nathan even in such vague outline. "That's my son," I say.

"How old is he?" Walter says.

"Twelve."

"My boy's only a little older than that. Fourteen. You wait. He'll turn on you then. They all do."

To get to Walter's house in the Duboce Triangle, I will have to drive through the narrow streets of Victorians in Noe Valley, over one hill and then another, to arrive at streets of dark storefronts locked behind iron grills and shabby-windowed apartment buildings. The city is so pretty, its softly folded hills offering such astonishing vistas, cupping miniature worlds in each valley, that it always comes as a shock to emerge into a pocket of poverty like Walter's neighborhood. It's mean of him to make me drop him off last; I have to lock all the doors as I drive back alone on streets where drunks collect like moths in the glow of corner liquor stores.

I look again at the windows of my house. I can't see Nathan's shadow anymore. I can't see any shadows behind the blank, translucent eyelids of the window shades. For a minute it seems as if I've only imagined the life I know goes on inside that house, belongs to me, welcomes me back.

"Can we go now?" I say.

"You can do whatever you want," Walter says.

When I get up from bed after we make love, Jay puts earplugs in his ears so I won't wake him when I come in later, a practical precaution that invokes guilt more effectively than a protest would. At my computer, I'll feel the pull of his wanting me to stay in bed, of his sane dismay at my foolish late hours and the price I'll pay tomorrow when I drag myself through the day. The four golden rules of AA are that you never allow yourself to stay hungry, angry, lonely, or tired. HALT.

I used to have to stay up later than Jay. When I was drinking, this was my chance to indulge without witnesses, devour stolen pleasure. When the bottle was empty, I'd exchange it for a full one from the case I kept hidden in the garage. I'd open the new bottle and pour off the equivalent of the glass or two I'd had with dinner, so that when Jay opened the fridge in the morning, the bottle would be there, telling a lie for me. I used to imagine that he observed me that carefully, that I had so much work to do to hide my secret.

Now I have nothing to hide except for the handouts on grammar that I type for my students while the house hums with silence. I print out the night's work on the computer, and then I click on the solitaire game. You can't cheat at solitaire on the computer. I've learned little strategic tricks: I never draw from the deck if I can move a faceup card and turn over the card beneath it instead. But chance determines whether each game is a process of slowly dwindling options or unexpected, expanding possibilities. I cannot quit until I've won three games. Even if my eyes grow heavy lidded with drowsiness, I have to keep playing, out of a narrow need so simple that I can vanish into it.

As usual Walter arranges things so that he'll be the last person I drop off. When we arrive in front of his house, he doesn't get out of the car. He asks if I'd mind if he has a cigarette before he goes.

We smoke together, watching the men who stand outside the corner liquor store, clutching brown paper bags twisted tight around the necks of bottles. It is cold enough that their breaths form clouds, unfurling so thick and white I'm reminded of smoke pluming from a locomotive, from some indefatigable engine of misery. The cloud of smoke in my car is tinged with the smell of gasoline that always clings to Walter, who nowadays is lucky to have a job pumping gas. This secret commingling of odors reminds me of my mother, who came home from work smelling of chocolate, a stale, cloying odor that should have been sweet but wasn't.

"I sure could go for a nice cold beer," Walter says.

"I only drank wine. Good California white wine."

"You lie right and left," Walter says. "Bullshit you only drank wine. Never had a desperate moment when you drained the cough syrup."

"Would you give me a break? I already have a complex about my piss-poor drunk credentials. I never have any big confessions to make at meetings."

"No. You're always so full of sweetness and light. Why do you put that on for all the other drunks? Like they don't know the scam."

"What do you want me to do? Apologize for being happy?"

Walter unlatches the door and heaves it open with a grunt, as if it requires superhuman effort. "You're not happy," he says.

Hannah has to make up word problems for her math homework. I help her count the books on the shelves in the bedrooms, the living room, my basement office, so that she can write a problem that requires adding all these sums. When she sits at her desk to arrange the numbers in a column to solve her own problem, we are both astonished to discover we own over twelve hundred books. I grew up in an apartment where there were no books, and I'm a materialist about them now, rarely use the library because I want to own what I covet. I stuff my children with these goodies, so essential to the sweet universe in which I want them to grow.

With my books, with Bach and Coltrane and Haydn, with the music and theater that Jay loves, I've accumulated enough wealth to insure me against the shabby rooms of my childhood, become a giddy nouveau riche of culture. So much so that when we have my mother to dinner she is puzzled, merely querulous in her poking: *Your hair's so black, do you dye it? That boy eats too much. Hannah's a fresh one, she is.* I feel as if I've put one over on her, Hansel putting a knuckle through the bars of the cage for the witch to pinch, hiding from her how fat I've grown on plenty.

Nathan pokes his head in the door to annoy his sister. I get up, slip the scarf from my neck, and lash it through the air like a lion tamer's whip, backing him into his room again. At the sound of his laughter, Hannah jumps up from her desk to join us, and the three of us are tangled on the floor when Jay comes home from work.

Jay gets down on his hands and knees with us, butting Hannah with his head and lowing like a cow, sneaking a feel on me in the tangle of bodies, kissing me in a showy way that the children pretend to be embarrassed by but that they really enjoy. Walter's wrong. Happiness is the simplest, most literal thing, as carelessly sprawled around me as the warm bodies of my three loves.

Walter is jumpier than usual, maybe because at the meeting tonight he confessed to backsliding, having a beer at a bar on his way home from work yesterday. We've gotten into the habit now of having two or three cigarettes together when I'm parked in front of his apartment building, and Walter can't sit still even when he's sitting still. He snaps the cover of his matchbook open and shut over and over, knocks his hand against the window while he talks, smears a spilled cake of ash into his clothing, tugs an oily strand of hair loose from his ponytail, raps a knuckle against the dashboard and scatters more flakes of ash there.

He asks me to come up to his apartment, just for a minute. "Just till I make sure the bogeyman isn't lying in wait."

I know better. I know he's come up with that bogeyman in order to trigger a maternal yes. Still I agree to come up.

His apartment is no surprise: an L-shaped studio with a garage-sale Formica table and two chairs next to the compact, filthy kitchen counter, a worn sofa covered with an ugly afghan. I could even say I feel at home with the bare floor, the bare walls, the big TV—a big blank eye, the only new thing. Clothes are scattered everywhere, and cups and plates. Beside the TV is a pyramid of crumpled, empty potato-chip bags. To make room for us to sit, he shovels things from the sofa—a blanket and pillow, a Game Boy, and a plate of stale crackers.

If I sit down, I'll have to stay. "Is that your kid's Game Boy?"

He nods. "I'm supposed to get my kid every other weekend. But he doesn't want to come anymore. Guess he doesn't like sleeping on the pullout sofa. My ex-wife won't help me out with him, either."

"Is that why—"

"There's always a reason," Walter says.

"You'd think she'd want him to have a relationship with his father."

Walter laughs. "Well, *you* might."

He lights another cigarette, and when he cups his hands around the match, the glow reflected on his face shivers like his shaking hands.

"I didn't always stick to wine," I say. "Sometimes I'd drink vodka."

Walter nods.

"When we went on trips. I used to dread vacations. I'd have to wash out bottles of shampoo and conditioner so I could refill them with vodka. And it still tasted like perfume. Jay would complain that he didn't see why I needed all those cosmetics when we were only going up to Lake Tahoe to sit on the beach. He still thinks that I never drank *that* much."

"It's hard not to develop a little contempt for people when you're an experienced drinker. The way they always want to be fooled."

"I always felt I was just about to be caught. That I had to be so careful."

"I remember that," Walter says. "Planning everything. So you could pretend you were in control." He holds out his shaking hands. His cigarette butt shivers between his trembling fingers. "Would you look at me now? Sometimes I wonder what the point is of staying sober. I'm never going to want anything—not a woman, not my son back—like I want a drink."

If Jay hasn't gone to sleep, he'll be starting to worry about why I'm late. "You should talk to your sponsor."

He smirks at me. "Take it through the appropriate channels."

"Maybe he can help you negotiate with your wife."

"My wife. She used to hide the car keys when I got drunk at home, 'cause once I reached a certain point, I'd want to go out and catch my buddies at the bar. She'd hide them in my kid's room when she put him to bed. I'd go in and turn on the light and start tossing his room. And she'd be on the bed with him, crying, and I'd grab her by the neck and start pushing her around the room. If I was looking in the wrong place, she'd have to say I was cold. If I was getting close, she'd have to say I was getting warm. Hot, hotter, hottest till I found the keys."

Walter places a shaking hand on my wrist.

"Will you be OK now?" I say. "I should really go."

Walter shrugs. "Aren't you at least going to look under the bed and behind the curtains before you go?"

The alcove that serves as his bedroom is so dim I can barely make out the outline of the bed, the concave surface of the lousy mattress.

He plucks at my wrist, so delicately. "That's another thing," he says. "I can't go to bed now, not if I'm alone. It's just so much work when you're stone-cold sober. I usually wake up on the sofa with the TV still going."

I know that everything everyone in AA confesses is genuine. I know that Roberta joined because one night she left a cigarette burning and destroyed her apartment, everything in it, and was lucky to escape with her own life and her son's. I can picture Walter's frightened wife, speaking her lines—"you're getting warmer"—wincing, dangling from his big, clamped hand. But Roberta has held me in her arms. Walter's touch now is so light that I want to press my mouth to the palm of his hand and kiss it. Walter, Roberta, all my fellow drunks, are like nesting boxes to me, one confession snugly fitted within another—the sad enclosing the brutal enclosing the next smaller universe of regret.

It's hard not to feel blue when I come home from another session with Walter. He wants me to come upstairs every time now, and I don't want to go, but I do. Jay is waiting up for me, sitting at the dining room table with a book. He always reads as if he's studying, with a certain grim sense of duty and discomfort, slogging away at the painful process of decoding words to get pleasure.

He slaps his book shut. "What's going on?" he says. "You come home later and later from your meetings."

"I just have so many people to give rides to." The habit of lying resurfaces so easily, and I want to blame Jay for this, for all the years when he so readily accepted excuses and pretexts.

"I was expecting you," Jay says. "I let Hannah wait up for you till nine-thirty."

I feel guilty as charged. Why do I not come home right away?

Why do I stay up at night, my eyes shutting against my will, staring at the cards on the green background of the solitaire screen? Why can't I say no to Walter when he leads me up the stairs to his apartment, badgers me inside with his darting hands?

When I offer no excuse, Jay says quietly, "I wish you'd be home with us more, that's all."

"Honey, I'm tired," I say. "Can we hash this over some other time?"

He gets up from the table and kisses me. "Come to bed then."

I'm amazed at how easily he yields. Grateful. We're both spared the alternative, the truncated binary series that stops at *no*, at confrontation. I can hardly be homesick for that, can I? I got my fill of it growing up, my whole childhood choked in the vise of my mother's misery and anger. But still, Jay's too easy, makes me feel I'll tumble forever through his transparent *yes*.

I tell Jay that I'm going to read for a while. "I need to wind down a little before I can sleep."

He sighs but doesn't protest. "Well, look in on Hannah. I promised you'd go in and kiss her even if she fell asleep."

I sneak into Hannah's room. I envy her for being able to sleep so open to the world, her arms spread wide. When I lean down to kiss her, her eyes fly open for a moment, and she murmurs "Mommy" and puts her arms up automatically.

"Good night, Peanut," I say, holding her limp body for a moment, knowing that she isn't really awake, that I've crossed the permeable barrier into her dreams, that my touch will be woven into them. I will never be so close to anyone, not even her own older self, as I am to her now, at this moment, when she has yet to outgrow the passionate possessiveness of her love for me. Nathan has already ordered me not to call him Little Guy anymore. One by one their nicknames will be crossed off each of their lists. I hold her for a moment longer to stave off the letting go that awaits us. Maybe that future already infuses the present, just as the past, when I could have lost my children or hurt them because of my addiction, compacts joy from the other direction.

I sit on the sofa reading long after Jay goes to bed. But I can't concentrate. Tonight Walter begged me to stay until he fell asleep. He took my hand, led me to the lumpily made bed. He said, "Please, just sit," but he was forcing me, in the same way he makes it impossible for me to say no to coming up to his apartment. He crawled under the covers in his clothes, held me there with a hard hand I could believe he raised against his wife, making a fist the way his tense body made a fist in the rumpled sheets. I could smell his unwashed hair, the stinging echo of gasoline fumes, and some mysterious sweetness I couldn't name. That vapor held me where I was, even though every muscle in my body tensed against the intimate closeness of his, the slithering commotion of his limbs beneath the blankets. I couldn't yank my hand from his or refuse when he asked me to lie down for just a minute, unfold my body from its determined resistance.

Now I'm filled with craving. Not for a drink. For something that there's always going to be more of. It cycles inside me like a piston, this want that has no object.

Walter calls me at school, claiming it's an emergency so the receptionist will fetch me from the classroom to take the phone. I don't even register what it is he wants, only know the compulsion to stave off the next demand by answering yes to this one. I make an excuse to the receptionist about a sick child and drive over to his apartment.

When Walter opens the door, dressed only in sweatpants, I see that he's cleaned up for me. The pile of crumpled chip bags is gone, there are no clothes on the floor, the narrow coffee table bears the streaks of a hasty swipe with a dust rag. Straightened up, this place is even uglier, more frightening to me. Through the partly closed curtains, light slants into the room like a blade.

"You can't call me in the middle of the day," I say.

"I need to sleep," he says. "I haven't slept for two days."

I follow him into the alcove, where he pulls back the untouched covers, climbs into bed, and pats the mattress next to him. I lie down beside him, and he pulls the sheets up over both of us, curls his body against mine.

He strokes my hair, and I can feel the warmth of him along my body, the oppressive clamminess of his sweat, his hot breath. A shock, like the nick of a static shock, runs through me each time he lifts my hair and lets it cascade over his hands. I can't believe the impossible fact of a man other than Jay caressing me. I shut my eyes, block out the light the way Jay's earplugs block the sound of me slipping into the bedroom after he's gone to sleep.

Walter's hand moves down over my shoulders, along my hip, where even through my clothes, it kindles an unpleasant warmth. The blunt ridge of his erection presses against my thigh, and then he shifts his hand to his own crotch, rubs himself in rhythmic circles that make his breath catch. I keep my body rigid, as if there's some rule that I must remain untouched, unmoved, while he does what he needs to do to arrive at release, to sprawl against me with a new, helpless softness. Soon I will have worked the magic that will enable him to sleep till morning comes, enable me to get up and fetch my children, move through the clean corridors of my own life, blunt the pleading of his fingers on my skin, renounce the complicity of our bodies rocking on the mattress.

After a while, when his breathing becomes even, I slip slowly and carefully from beneath the covers. I need to leave him sleeping, need to lean over him to tuck the sheets around him in just the way I would tuck them around my children. Only when he's asleep do I want or dare to touch him, brush damp hair back from his forehead.

His hand comes up like a vise to grip mine in the act of tenderness. Panic bolts through me when he pulls me down toward the bed.

"Please," he says, "just one little good-night kiss."

He shifts his hand to the back of my neck, brings my face to his. The pressure of Walter's mouth on mine unlocks an answer, and I open my mouth to let his tongue fill the little cave of my hunger.

He laughs when I jerk back from the bed. "Sweet dreams," he says, as if I am the one he has released to oblivion.

I race down the stairs as if he will come after me. When I get into my car, I lock the doors, but I can't turn the key in the ignition, not with these hands. I look in the rearview mirror, see that my lipstick is smeared around my mouth. I spit into a Kleenex and slowly rub the rosy aura from my skin. I run my fingers through the disarray of my hair, hiding the evidence once again.

But it's there in the gaze the mirror reflects. I'm not the only one in the world with the eyes of a liar. No, there's a herd of us, the comrades of lonely craving, slapping down folding chairs in a thousand musty meeting rooms. I close my eyes the way I closed them when Walter kissed me, and again I can feel the rushing warmth of desire, of hungered-after contact. Such allegiance it claims, this second self, this scavenger who returns to demand its sweet share, whom I must let come and go, come and go, move through me like fog.

honor among thieves

Three days after Daniel left Carrie, a tree came down against her house in a terrible rainstorm, crushing the front stairs and puncturing the roof. Carrie and her daughter, Anya, got up from bed and set out buckets, every last pot and pan in the kitchen, even piles of rags, to catch the water sluicing down the walls, dripping from cracks in the ceiling. Yanking the sofa and armchair away from the seeping walls, Carrie thought that it was just as well that Daniel had taken a lot of the furniture. In the morning she ripped the heavy water-soaked curtains from the living-room windows, sending the curtain hooks pinging across the bare wood floor, and bundled the curtains into the trash. She was glad to strip the house, toss ruined rugs, empty the mantel of her collection of Talavera pottery, survey the water stains on the walls as if they were destruction's bold scrawl, writ large.

For two weeks she and Anya have been stepping over the bowls and pots and pans on the floor, curling together in Carrie's bed, the only place in the house that stays dry when it rains. The landlord has cleared away the fallen tree but made excuses about repairing the roof and the front steps, claiming that every roofing contractor he calls is busy because of all the rain this winter. He has left the house in disrepair for years, hoping to force Carrie out so he can jack up the rent.

When Foster brings Anya home on Sunday night, he climbs in the window after her—they can't use the front steps. Carrie has spent the day in her robe, left her hair in a tangled spill down her back. She wasn't expecting him to come in with Anya.

Foster lifts a corner of the drop cloth she's thrown over the furniture huddled in the middle of the room. "You've got to snap out of this," he says.

He is perfectly confident, as Carrie is, that the damage is her doing. Anya must report to her father and stepmother when she spends the weekend with them: Mom's not cooking, she's living on candy bars, she's not sleeping. Carrie can live with Foster thinking she is crazy. But her eyes cross at the thought of another lecture from him on the needs of a teenager.

Carrie shrugs. "I can't help this mess."

"You're wallowing in it," Foster says. "There'll be someone else soon enough."

"Dad," Anya scolds automatically.

Should Carrie be flattered or dismayed at Foster's expectation? She's been thinking that there won't be another someone for a while. When she split up with Foster twelve years ago, she was so certain of what she was leaving him for. Yes, she was going to fall in love, desperately, pursue her dream of working as an artist, live in a neighborhood that offered noise and struggle, not hushed, propertied order. She's had one adventure after another since she left Foster, scrabbling together waitressing jobs until she found the job at the frame shop, falling in and out of love so many times, fighting the landlord because if she had to pay higher rent, she couldn't afford to sublet studio space two days a week.

"You should move out," Foster says.

"The roofer is supposed to come next week," Carrie says.

"That's what you said last weekend."

She gives him a look. But Foster persists. "I know a good handyman. I could get him in here to fix those front steps for you—"

"We like going in and out the window," Carrie says. "Anya just calls for me when she gets home from school. 'Rapunzel, Rapunzel, let down your hair.'"

"Look, my daughter has to live here," Foster says.

"Don't put me in the middle," Anya says. But her voice has an impish lilt; she likes to best them at the game of being a grown-up.

"Oh, Foster," Carrie says. "Will you just relax? After the roofer gets here, I'll paint the walls. We'll just be so shipshape and middle class you won't know us."

Anya comes into the bedroom and tugs open the curtains. The sudden light makes Carrie feel as if her pupils are made of chips of glass, refracting and distorting what she sees: the mildewed square on the wall where Daniel's bureau used to stand, the paper bags of clothes that have taken the place of the bureau drawers, the dusty mess of the vanity table with its filmy mirror.

Anya yanks the blankets off Carrie's body. "You have to go to work."

"We stayed up too late," Carrie moans.

"You drank too much," Anya says.

Carrie tries to remember. They sat on the sofa together, their legs in each other's laps, eating popcorn and watching a video, *Some Like It Hot*, with Marilyn Monroe managing to be so calculating and so innocent all at the same time that of course you wanted her to get the rich man she was angling for. Carrie leaned down now and then to refill her glass from the bottle of wine on the floor. Now and then.

"I'm entitled to suffer," Carrie says.

Anya swats her. "Get over yourself, Mom. He's been gone for a month."

"Is that any way to speak to your mother?" Carrie says. But she swings her legs over the side of the bed. "Make coffee. Please?"

Carrie gets dressed in clothes that will make her feel better, a long, diaphanous skirt, a see-through blouse with a tank top underneath, chunky heels. Hardly clothes she ought to wear to the frame shop. Her boss has been riding her about her erratic hours, which has only made her more persistently tardy. Her work is good—the shop does frames for galleries, for half the artists out at Hunters Point where Carrie has her studio, and a lot of the customers request her when they come in because she's decisive, has a trustworthy instinct for simplicity, is efficient with materials.

She sits at the vanity table and fishes among tiny compacts filled with delicious creamy colors that she can't resist. She may have the largest collection of makeup in the city of San Francisco, a collection to rival a drag queen's. Her hangover gives her some technical problems. Her hand shakes when she applies blush, and it takes two attempts to apply eyeliner. When she reapplies it, one finger stretching the eyelid, she can't help noticing that wrinkles make the job harder too. She's exactly of an age, forty-three, to feel shocked that her body is no longer young, no longer a match for the firmness of her desire.

And maybe this is why she counted on Daniel, crossed her fingers during their four years together—her longest time with any man since Foster—and didn't see how little that meant to Daniel, who did not have behind him the string of failed relationships that she did. Six years younger, his life still as flexible as his skin, he never questioned the opportunity that beckoned in New York. And she'd had to choose: accuse and make their last months miserable or corroborate in the lie that fate was separating them, severing their great passion. She'd gone with the lie.

The tattoo on her shoulder, a heart with an arrow through it, shows through her translucent blouse. Daniel's name is inscribed on the shaft of the arrow, crude and shameless epithet. She and Daniel argued unscrupulously and savagely, made up with sex predictably but gorgeously stoked by their anger, stuffed each other's pockets with vulgar love notes folded into stiff origami shapes. They fought to keep alive their infatuation, clung to its absolute diction despite his irresponsibility and hers. Her marriage to Foster had taught her the price of accommodation.

Anya comes back and kisses Carrie's cheek when she leans down to place a steaming mug on the vanity table. Carrie hands Anya her hairbrush, and Anya pulls up a stool behind Carrie's chair.

Carrie used to brush Anya's hair for hours every day, and now that Anya has cropped her hair close around her face, the better to show off the three holes pierced in each ear, they have reversed places. But Anya hesitates at her task. She says, "You *will* make it to work today, won't you, Mom?"

The night of the big storm, when they were running around setting out pots and pans to catch the dripping water, barefoot, in their nightgowns, Carrie and Anya finally gave up their hopeless effort. Carrie salvaged a pot to make hot chocolate, and when water dripped from the ceiling into the boiling milk, Carrie started to cry and then to laugh, and she and Anya laughed so hard they had to hold on to each other.

"Of course," Carrie says. "The world of art would grind to a halt without me."

She'll call in sick. She just can't explain to Anya, still a child, or to herself this helplessness, this inexplicable, self-dramatizing need to stay put, to be bereft.

Slowly the progress of the brush turns smooth as a caress. Both of them luxuriate in the wordless intimacy of this ritual, this lover-like intentness. Though she stayed with Foster for three more years, Carrie knew when Anya was born that she didn't really love him, knew because her feelings for Foster were nothing like the aching physical need she felt for her daughter. Carrie had been terrible to Foster, bluntly instructing him not to bore her with his work stories, vengefully spending the money he made as an orthopedic surgeon on expensive clothes and Oriental rugs and paintings he didn't like, and toward the end taking lovers. Still, he didn't believe her when she said she wanted to separate, forced her through three months of marriage counseling before he let her go.

Foster wanted Carrie to stay in their house with Anya, keep it as her share of community property. She told him to sell it. Carrie could not take Foster's money anymore, could not help a sense of honor at the last, even if it was akin to the honor among thieves.

Carrie can hear the carpenter hammering on the front steps. It's really Foster hammering at her, Foster who hired the guy and told him to show up—surprise!—on Carrie's doorstep. Her first impulse was to send the carpenter away, call Foster's office, and light into him for trying to run her life. But the carpenter, Matt, turned out to be cute, and the window they'd been using as an entryway was beginning to stick from all the water damage. Maybe the carpenter will loan her his tools; the roofer who showed up put more cracks in the ceiling and walls with his heavy equipment. Maybe Carrie is worse off than she thinks she is if Foster is willing to risk interfering. They've always operated under a laissez-faire policy— she keeps her mouth shut when Foster sends Anya to his horrible parents for holiday visits, and Foster forebears comment on Carrie's lax rules, Anya's stories of meeting strange men in the bathroom in the morning. Carrie will paint the living room as soon as she can repair the cracks in the walls.

Matt stops hammering, turns off his radio. A moment later he pokes his head in the door. "I think I'm going to head out," he says. "There's some nasty dry rot under the steps. I can't fix it until I buy more lumber."

"Liar." He likes to leave early to go the beach, carries a surfboard and wet suit in his truck even in winter. He's young.

He smiles, unashamed. "Mind if I wash up?" he says.

She follows him into the kitchen, offers him a drink. Today she should have gone to the studio at Hunters Point. She is lucky that Edward lets her share his space for a pittance. Usually she shows up religiously on her days off from the frame shop, Thursdays and Fridays, exercising a discipline and self-sacrifice she expends on nothing else, summoning the will to persist in failure, which has required so much more loyalty than success would have.

Matt turns the water on full blast and lathers his arms up to the elbows till they look as if they've been dipped in cream. Carrie has found herself skipping the studio with the excuse that she'll draw at home just so she can look out the window to spy on him, bicker with him about his noise and his hours. How weak she is, to crave beautiful men so, to give in to this secret indulgence, luscious and painful. And this pleasure is laced with a kind of panic that she will fail to feel every delightful increment of sensation, the same panic that makes her knot her body, kernel hard, and force herself to think of Daniel, remember touching him, recall the way he slumped over his coffee in the morning, painstakingly reconstruct the contour of his cheek, the faceted knobs of his knuckles, the ways of his body and no one else's.

Drying his hands on a towel, Matt glances surreptitiously at her face and then looks away. He's too young not to be embarrassed, priggish about the possibility that she could be sending him sexual signals.

Warmth blooms in her body at this tempting resistance. She reaches up to tuck a bra strap under her tank top, to draw his eyes to her shapely shoulder.

"Can I borrow a putty knife from you?" she says. "And Spackle, if you have it?"

He blushes, rich reward for her first, virtuous small step.

Foster saved Carrie's life. When they were first married, they traveled together a lot, a frivolity Foster can still afford regularly and Carrie cannot. When he finished his residency, they drove down to Baja, Mexico, to celebrate. They camped on the beach, rose with the sun every morning to make cowboy coffee in a pot precariously perched over their small fire, throwing the grounds into the boiling water, straining the coffee through a cloth, and then thickening the weak brew with sweetened condensed milk. They were hiking, miles from the nearest village, when she got stung by a bee and went into anaphylactic shock. Foster made an incision in her throat with a Swiss Army knife, an emergency tracheotomy, had the courage and the steadiness to do what was necessary. He carried her over a mile back to their car, drove her, with her head resting in his lap, into the village to a dilapidated hospital. For years they showed slides of their trip to friends, the show always culminating with slides of the Baja beach, the story of how Foster saved Carrie's life on that day.

When Foster shows up at her Open Studio at Hunters Point, Carrie can't help feeling that he has turned up to rescue her again, and that it's her own fault. She'd told him she would agree to the carpenter only if she could pay Foster back after her upcoming Open Studio, intimated that she could count on selling canvases and making some real money. And now she'll never again be able to allude vaguely to her studio space, her work, without Foster knowing exactly what that means: a poor-cousin corner of Edward's space, a grand total of six canvases to show. She may well be fired for the sake of those six canvases. When she asked for the day off today, her boss told her not to bother coming in next week.

Foster bumps against her easel and rights it. Then he announces that it's about time he owned an original Carrie Decker.

"Spare me the paternalism," Carrie says. "Nobody's even come in to look."

"Maybe you scared them off," Foster says. "Look at you! Your hair's a mess, and did you know that your shoes don't match?"

Carrie looks at her feet. One boot is brown, one black. Well, she was tired this morning. She couldn't sleep last night, called Daniel at 3 A.M. New York time, listened in panic to the phone ring and ring—maybe she'd memorized a wrong number, maybe he was sleeping somewhere else—until she heard him say "hello?" into the phone, into her silence, his voice blessedly familiar, his sleepy bewilderment so intimate.

"Are you all right?" Foster says.

"I'm an artist," Carrie says. "I get to be this way."

He brushes a strand of hair from her face and then draws back from her.

She can feel it, like some chemical reaction, the tense stillness of his response to her physical proximity. It's no different from the wariness that makes Matt, the carpenter, rock on his heels when Carrie steps too close to him, envelops him in the tantalizing aura of her grief, her preoccupation with someone who isn't him.

"Lisa's here somewhere," Foster says, as if he has to remind them both of his wife. "She'll turn up eventually. So tell me which picture we should buy."

Carrie follows him as he moves along the wall, squinting at the stickers that list the title and price of each canvas. He stops before the largest canvas, her most recent one. "'Dream House.' You've done a series of houses, haven't you?"

"It's inspired by my recent travails," Carrie says. "My next series is going to be called 'Black Holes.'"

"Oh, stop being so maudlin." Foster takes her elbow lightly, calling up for her so suddenly and fully her favorite thing about him, the professional, precise lightness of his touch. He can feel bruised skin for a broken bone without giving pain. His gentleness makes her want to burst into tears.

"Tell me about this picture," he says.

She explains how she painted washes of color, one translucent layer over another, to build up a thick but seamless layer of paint that suggests a doll's house, rooms stacked above each other. She glued on tiny squares of paper, cut from gift wrap, from a letter Daniel wrote her (robbed of any power once she put it to use), from the green foil cups in a box of chocolates. Then she built up more thin washes of paint to shellac the squares, embed them in the surface of the canvas.

She sticks to giving Foster a technical description. She's been painting houses because she has a recurring dream about a house, one that predates even her current disastrous circumstances. Always she is walking through beautiful, empty rooms, an endless profusion of them, imagining how she will fill them when she and Anya move in. It ought to be a happy dream, but she never wakes up from it happy.

"I think I'd like to take this one," Foster says.

She suspects the offer is made out of charity, not desire. "It's not finished."

"Sure it is," Foster says. "You hung it and priced it."

A few days ago, when this canvas was still on her easel, she couldn't decide whether to scrape into those layers of paint with a palette knife or to build them up further, stroke on opaque paint that would retain the imprint of the brush hairs. All the determination, the boldness, that made her so damn cheery when she was in the early stages abruptly deserted her at the end.

Working on a canvas, Carrie always arrives at this moment of regret, of complete doubt in her ability to recognize the mistakes she has made. Her hand will wander to the vertical scar of the tracheotomy like a tongue to an aching tooth.

When Lisa arrives, Foster steps away from Carrie so that she can stand between them. "Isn't this great?" He sweeps an arm as if all the canvases on the wall are his.

"It's really neat," Lisa says. "We've never come to an Open Studio before. All these artists in one place!"

Carrie has no right to her inward sneer. Those are her feelings exactly—excitement and awe at the idea of being an artist, being among artists. She was disappointed to find herself alone so often on her days here. The beautiful light that's to be had in these converted warehouses, so close to the bay, comes at a compounded price: most of the tenants have to work day jobs to pay the rent, and the land is steeped in poison from the years when this was a Navy shipyard.

Foster and Lisa glance at Carrie for signs of disapproval every time they dare to comment on a picture. Carrie wraps her hands more tightly around herself and gives them only a vindictive stare that their polite effort does not deserve. When she left Foster, she accused him of not supporting her as an artist, and he said, "I always encouraged you," using the word that made her feel like a doctor's wife with a hobby. Lisa, so anonymously attractive, so varnished, makes a much better wife for him.

Foster pulls his checkbook from his pocket. "Do I add tax to the total?"

The music has been turned up so loud that Carrie can feel the bass beat through her bare feet, a pump driving the bodies crowded into her living room. In the ocher light cast by the one lamp left in the room, the dancers' undulating shadows lick at the walls like tongues of dark flame. Someone climbs back in through the open living-room window—people have been climbing in and out all night, since the stairs are still under construction—bringing in a whiff of sweet smoke. Carrie makes her friends smoke pot outside, out of sight of Anya, as a concession to maternal duty. She doesn't smoke pot herself because it induces lethargy, though you'd never know it from the way her friends behave.

She is drunk enough to feel transcendent, as benevolent as if she has personally orchestrated the chaos around her: the blender whirring in the kitchen where people are making daiquiris, two people sketching in pencil on the scarred walls, someone sleeping on the sofa, still draped with the drop cloth, someone else twirling the standing lamp so the light swims across the wall and ceilings, and yet another someone lighting sparklers that hiss and spit, parting the closely packed dancers. Carrie barely knows half the people here, just collected whoever was available at the end of the Open Studio, waving Foster's check to prove she could provide plenty of free liquor.

She lets Edward drape his arms around her for a slow dance, contemplates the possibility of taking him into her bed later tonight. They occasionally sleep together, a just-friends kind of thing in which they both acknowledge each other as temporary stopgaps, and she is feeling so lonely, roused to such craving by the daily, muscular presence of the carpenter. But Anya will scold her. Anya has already come over to her once to wean her away from Edward and hiss in her ear, "Mom, how can you be so promiscuous in the age of AIDS?"

Carrie looks for Anya and is relieved to find her sitting cross-legged in the corner talking to Marty, who has the studio next to Edward's at Hunters Point. Carrie trusts Marty not to prey on Anya. She trusts herself, the self she imagines tugging the invisible strings that coordinate every body in this room, suspending everyone in the dreamy blissfulness of loud music and dimness and movement.

When Anya collars her to tell her there's a neighbor at the window, complaining about the noise, Carrie shrugs. She doesn't want to be bothered. She refuses to go to the window to speak to the neighbor.

"Do you want him to call the cops?" Anya demands.

"Oh, he won't." Carrie loops an arm around Anya's waist, tries to draw her into a circle with Edward. "Isn't my baby beautiful?"

Anya pushes at Carrie's arm. "Mom, can you get serious?"

"You're the one who told me I should lighten up," Carrie says.

Anya goes back to the neighbor at the window. "It's my mother's party," Anya says loudly. "I can't do anything about it. I'm just a kid."

There is such amusement in Anya's voice that Carrie doesn't suspect anything when she sees Anya dig the phone out from under the drop cloth and sit on the windowsill with the receiver to her ear. Later, when a loud banging on the window scatters the crowd in her living room, funneling people into the kitchen to head out the back door, Carrie thinks that the neighbor did call the police. She is stunned when Foster compresses his tall body to squeeze in through the window.

Anya is waiting with her backpack in hand, a preparation Carrie should have noticed. Someone calls from the kitchen to ask if it's the cops, and Carrie turns off the CD player and answers, "No. It's just the lifestyle police."

Foster puts his hands up defensively. "Anya asked me to come get her."

The flannel collar of a pajama top sticks up from beneath his windbreaker. Carrie laughs. "Jesus, Foster, you wear pajamas now?"

"Don't be mad at me, Mom," Anya says. "I just wanted some sleep. I have to study for a test on Monday."

"Of course I'm not mad, honey," Carrie says. "You do what you want." She turns back to Foster. "You're welcome to stay for a drink."

"Look at this mess," Foster says. "You have to get hold of yourself. We're going to have to talk."

"I hate your talks," Carrie says. He always arranges to meet on what he has decided is neutral territory, some coffee shop where he will be so fucking civilized, polite and hands-off and judgmental.

"Fine," Foster says. "That's just fine."

He backs out the window, and Anya goes after him, stuffing her backpack through ahead of her. Carrie leans out the window to watch them go to the car. Anya looks back once, ducking her head as if she expects a blow, some curse to land on her. And Carrie hopes the party will last all night, because she realizes only as Anya gets into the car that she was looking forward, after everyone left, to having Anya lead her to bed, pull off her shoes, maybe even sit quietly in her room and talk.

Foster keeps catching her. Before Carrie even catches herself doing what she's doing. She and Matt are in bed when she hears a noise at the front of the house. Though the steps are repaired, the front door is off its hinges so Matt can shave the warped wood at the bottom. She remembers too late that Foster had mentioned coming over to talk. She'd been so annoyed by the implicit criticism of his urgency, his violation of his own rule of neutrality, that she hadn't paid attention to when.

She jumps from the bed, throws on clothes, and finds Foster in the living room.

"I'm sorry I didn't knock," Foster says. He laughs. "But there isn't any door."

She tries to think. How did this happen? This morning she taped the baseboards and the trim on the windows in preparation for painting. She borrowed a ladder from Matt and returned the Spackle she'd used to repair the damaged walls. She put music on her CD player, poured paint into a tray, dipped a roller into its creaminess, stroked the paint onto the walls. The roller made a rhythmic, squishy sound, and those neat rectangular strips of clean new white transformed the discolored walls into blank pages. Some dread took hold of her. *I'm not going to be able to do this.*

She turned up the volume on her CD player to drown out Matt's radio on the front steps, to cover the sound of her crying. She brushed at her tears, smearing her cheeks with paint. Matt came in and took the roller from her. He ignored her tear-stained face. He let her run her hands over his, up over the sharp outcrop of his wrists and along the curves of his muscled arms.

In her bedroom, he shucked his clothes with the graceless, greedy haste of the young, gave no thought to being seen. She slipped from her clothes more surreptitiously, glad she hadn't ripped out the curtains in here. She could not help imagining what he might see: the creases and folds and puckering of flesh that had survived hard use for four decades, borne a child.

Matt comes out of the bedroom, dressed, but barefoot as Carrie is.

She should have warned him to stay in the room.

"Hey," Matt says to Foster, but he can't meet the eyes of the man who hired him. He turns to Carrie. "I'm going to head out, I think. I'll see you tomorrow."

He leaves quickly, silently, lightly, his shoes in his hand. What was it she thought she was doing in bed with Matt? After they made love, she lay in his arms, drawing a deep breath, letting loneliness back in, trying to see if she could fill her lungs with it, not have her breath catch on that thickness.

Foster clears his throat. "I see you've gotten over your heartbreak."

She's not still married to him, yet she can't look at him. Her hand floats up to cover the scar at her throat.

"I need to talk to you about Anya," Foster says. "I think she should stay with us for a couple of weeks while you get the house back in shape."

"Why? What for?"

"For God's sake, you don't even have a door."

Matt was supposed to put the door back on its hinges before he left. He must have forgotten—his mind on the beach, the next pleasure of the day—as soon as he crawled from her bed.

"That's temporary," Carrie says. "Look, Foster, I'm sorry about this—"

"It's none of my business," Foster says firmly.

Carrie can count on one hand the times she has found herself on Foster's doorstep. He always ferries Anya back and forth because Carrie doesn't have a car and his ritzy neighborhood near Sea Cliff is hard to reach by bus. She feels nervous when she rings the bell. She has never been desperate enough to cross Foster's threshold, and now Foster is the one who has all the leverage.

As soon as Foster lets her inside, he offers her a tour of the house. She is overwhelmed by the size of the foyer—big enough to hold three huge Japanese chests and still feel empty—and smacked anew by the fact that Foster is a wealthy man.

She holds out her hands before her, wrists together. "Just arrest me, officer, and let's get this over with."

He shakes his head. "I'm not having that kind of conversation with you."

"Where's Lisa? Doesn't she want to be here to lecture me too?"

"She's at work. Her job at the ad agency is very demanding. But I've got all the time in the world. Let me show you the house. At least have a look at where we hung your painting."

He leads her into the living room, sheer drapes drawn against the sun, two huge sofas facing each other before the stone fireplace, chests and shelves and tables laden with bric-a-brac, glass figurines, Chinese vases and bowls, and on the walls, dark oil paintings of prissy British countryside, even a fox hunt, in massive gilt frames. So much plunder. She's filled with a visceral contempt for desire dulled and drowned by its own profusion, the habit of accumulation. She shouldn't have come here. She shouldn't have let him blackmail her with Anya, shouldn't have furiously painted the walls, shoved the furniture back in place, talked her way back into her job. See, Foster? I'll be good.

"I want Anya to come home," Carrie says. "The house is fixed up now."

"I think she should live here. She's more comfortable here."

"She belongs with me."

Foster takes her elbow. "Foster, please," she says, moving into that gentle touch, so light yet so firm, so reliable.

"You don't even see how guilty she feels leaving you. You probably want her that way. Whatever will keep her comforting you and looking after you and making sure you get out of bed in the morning. You are so selfish."

She must be. Anyone who confuses her own need with necessity as often as she does must be selfish. Only selfishness could have led her to mistake Foster's concern for her as some vestigial grace left from the time when they did, must have, loved one another.

With gouging, goading politeness, Foster says, "Come on, there's more to see."

His hand, as mechanically accurate as a pincer, propels her into the dining room, dominated by a huge dark table so shiny it makes her think of a polished casket, then through the kitchen, so perfectly appointed, and into the family room. This room offers the first lovely thing she's seen here, if she excepts the Oriental rug in the dining room, a purchase she made long ago and left with Foster as ransom. A huge picture window opens onto a lush garden and an expansive, unobstructed view of the bay. The floweriness of this room—the pink-and-yellow chintz sofas, the lettuce green carpeting, the doll collection in a display case—pales before the magnificent window. Foster doesn't bother to point out her painting, which he somehow cheated her out of only so Lisa could hang it in a corner, in the least obtrusive spot she could find.

"I know this place is probably a bit precious for your taste," Foster says. "I keep telling Lisa to go easy on the pastels. But will you look at the view I've got?"

Carrie could have been living here in this house with him. Sometimes she boasted to her friends that she used to be married to a surgeon: I gave it all up. As if she'd done something noble.

She can't yank her arm free of his. "Foster, let go! You just want to punish me."

"You can handle that all by yourself," Foster says. "You're an expert at it."

He drags her up the stairs in that mysteriously unbreakable grip, and when she stumbles, he keeps pulling her. He shoves open the door of a bedroom. The twin bed, neatly made, covered by a hand-made quilt, must be Anya's. Anya never makes her bed at home, and Carrie and Anya have argued for years about her sloppiness. More sheer curtains, delicate jewelry boxes, a Matisse poster on the wall, a cluster of framed photographs on the bureau. This is the room of another girl, someone Carrie doesn't know. The photos prove it: pictures of the three of them, Foster, Lisa, and Anya, the reconstituted family in frames that Carrie knows Lisa picked out, Lisa filled. Proof. Those slide shows, the grand finale against which Carrie's own desires were nothing.

Foster has tempted her, finally, to feel longing, even if it is not the kind he wishes her to feel.

"I've put up with your irresponsibility for long enough," Foster says. "The way you rub my nose in it."

To remember the sweetness of that morning in Mexico, sharing the syrupy coffee from one tin cup, pains her as much as it does to owe him her life. There's no proof.

Her body moves to comfort him, reflexively, but he shifts his grip to keep her at arm's length.

"I want Anya to stay here," Foster says. "Any court would back me up."

"Don't do this," Carrie whispers. She tries again to touch him.

He pushes her against the wall with a fury she knows is her fault. "It's too late to be sorry now. But are you? Are you sorry?"

His face is so close to hers, their mouths only a few inches from a kiss. He trembles, pressed against her. She has used her body so carelessly and so often in the service of frantic, deluded hope, why shouldn't she barter it now for her daughter, her only child, her one true need?

"No," she says.

curled in the bed of love

'Their friends are not dropping like flies any-more. Now twenty-five pills a day will keep death from the door indefinitely. And all the medieval horrors—the purplish lesions of KS mottling the beautiful curve of a young man's calf, thrush growing thick as a furry pelt in a mouth that should have been kissed, a dark neck wound opening like an obscene portal—are no longer a daily fact of their lives.

Sometimes Jim imagines that his and Jordan's love has grown like the lush grass on all the graves they have each visited in the last decade. They met at an open grave. By that time the funerals had become as fantastic as the disease—a ceremony in a nightclub rented for the evening, a service conducted jointly by a rabbi and a Buddhist monk, a party where everyone said their good-byes to the host, whose flesh was evaporating from his bones by slow degrees.

At Michael's funeral, the mourners were asked to place in the grave some precious gift for him to take into the sweet afterlife. In single file, men lined up to drop onto the coffin a silk scarf, pages torn from a book of poetry, a pinecone, a Game Boy. Jordan was in line ahead of Jim. Jordan dropped into the grave a pair of eye-glasses, explained his awkward gift when Jim stepped up to deposit one perfect peach.

"He was so vain he wouldn't use his reading glasses," Jordan said. "When we went out to eat, somebody always had to read the menu to him."

Jordan's shoulders began to shake, and Jim put an arm around him and led him away. Back then, you took anyone in your arms at these things, for whoever grieved more intensely was only temporarily taking your place in the endlessly reshuffled hierarchy of mourners.

Jordan put his hands up to ward off Jim. "Don't," he said. "I'm not crying for him." He didn't have to confess he was seropositive.

After the service everyone met for lunch at a barbecue restaurant. Jim sat with Jordan, and they discovered they had nothing in common. Jordan was a partner in a small art gallery downtown, and Jim was a physical therapist. Their only mutual interest was their volunteer work in the AIDS ward at San Francisco General. But everyone did that in those days. The ward swarmed with boisterous volunteers who delivered flowers and library books, plumped pillows, told jokes, gave manicures, served the fancy Sunday brunches donated by restaurants and caterers.

Jim struggled to hold Jordan's attention. He met all kinds of people in his work, he said. "And you're touching their bodies, working them through pain. They tell you everything. The writers tell me their ideas for stories, the bankers give me tips on investing. I know more about them than their hairdressers do."

Jordan smiled politely, and Jim was thinking of excusing himself to sit with friends when Michael's cousin turned his video camera on them. Michael's cousin had been going from table to table, and now he wanted Jim to tell one story about Michael. Jim couldn't think of a story. All he could remember was that Michael was forever stepping in dog shit. He stared openmouthed at the camera. Instead of turning the punishing lens away, Jordan turned Jim's face to his, kept his hand cupped protectively along the line of Jim's jaw.

That gesture was all it took for Jim to fall for Jordan. Then, intimacy came quickly and fiercely. Jim, still healthy, never had to ask himself whether he really loved Jordan. What he fought down the first night they spent together, when he studied Jordan's unmarked body in the soft glow of a bedside lamp, imagined the raging disease already scarring organs and unseen tissue, was absolute proof in and of itself.

Now that time has unfurled before them again, a red carpet unrolled, they can handle a rough spot or two. Jordan has only just started back to work full-time after two years of devoting himself to his health. Jordan was lucky that he could afford the time off—thanks to his parents' determination to avoid inheritance taxes, he had enough capital sunk into the business that his partner had to accommodate him. How they celebrated his first day back—Jim sent Jordan flowers at the gallery with a card signed "J.J.," their nickname for each other, the twinned link of their initials, and served up a candlelight dinner when Jordan got home. But Jordan's been much more tired since he started back at the gallery. Jim worried at first, insisted Jordan go for a battery of blood tests. His T4 cell count is OK. He's just tired. Too tired to want more than a cuddle when they curl up in bed. For two years they've fallen asleep every night in the embrace of new love, spooned together with their arms entwined, but now, after a quick hug, Jordan rolls away from Jim into a sleep he needs so desperately that it must be solitary.

Usually Jordan invites artists he's interested in to dinner parties with seven or eight other people, so they'll be just one of the crowd. But Jordan invited Lawrence to dinner by himself, which means he wants the gallery to show Lawrence's work more than Lawrence does. Jim has been reduced to the role of quiet housewife, serving up chicken simmered with chickpeas and star anise, clearing dishes, bringing dessert on a tray to the living room, and then kneeling by the coffee table until the other two are willing to interrupt their study of Lawrence's portfolio of slides.

Lawrence and Jordan are talking about Paris, where to stay and where to eat cheaply, and sometimes they lapse into French, as if they've forgotten that Jim doesn't understand them. Even French words sound crude, scatological, coming out of Lawrence's mouth. He has an air of coarseness about him that inflects his speech, tangles the wild mass of his hair, shimmers in his sloppy gestures.

Lawrence says he plans to go to Paris later this spring.

"Maybe I should go when you're there," Jordan says. He used to go to Paris every year, before he got sick, before he met Jim.

Jim hasn't made the effort he should have to share Jordan's interests. But then there's the effort Jordan should make. Jim says, "You promised we'd go to Hawaii this spring."

Jordan turns to Lawrence, puts a hand on his wrist confidingly. "He wants to go to this place called Kona Village—Kontiki thatched huts and a pool where you lie around in swim trunks and drink piña coladas from coconut shells."

Jim has wanted to go back to Kona Village for a long time. Even if it was all put on for the tourists, he'd been captivated by how lazy life was there. "You'd look good lying around in swim trunks," he says to Jordan.

Lawrence gives Jordan a rudely appraising look. "I was gonna ask you what gym you go to."

The truth is, Jordan looks buff thanks to steroids. The AZT he's taking wastes muscle tissue almost as drastically as the disease, so the doctors automatically put everyone on steroids to beef up before the drug begins to make inroads.

"'Cause my gym . . . I don't know," Lawrence says. "It's such an autoerotic scene. Mirrors on every wall. Some of these guys get hard-ons looking at themselves on the Nautilus machine."

"Safe sex takes another turn for the worse," Jordan says.

Jordan has never looked so beautiful as he does now. There was a time, early in their relationship, when Jordan made Jim agree to help him die if it came to that. Such promises Jim made, lover's promises like no others. They considered smothering Jordan, debated whether plastic bags or pillows would be better, then thought maybe they could collect enough sleeping pills to do the job. Jim conned one doctor after another into prescribing Vicodin for back pain. It was *their* stockpile, *their* beautiful death: they joked about lighting candles and listening to a Bach concerto at their very own glorious send-off.

Lawrence reaches for his wine glass with a blunt paw. The glass tips over, threading red wine over the edge of the table onto the carpet, and Jim jumps up and runs for the saltshaker and a rag.

He shakes salt on the stain and blots it carefully, ignoring Lawrence's apology. It's an Oriental carpet, an heirloom from Jordan's family.

"You're such a hausfrau," Jordan says.

Jordan can afford to be casual about the plenty with which he grew up, has retained the habit of nonchalance even though the expense of surviving has transformed his wealth into a finite resource.

"That's me," Jim says. He rocks back on his heels, pinches the flesh at his waist between his fingers. "I've got my little matronly pudge, my apron for every day of the week. I sing along to *Miss Saigon* when I dust the furniture. A real fairy."

Jordan laughs. "OK, I had that coming." He blows Jim a kiss but speaks to Lawrence. "He wins every argument. He's got it down cold, that cute little *miffed* thing."

Jim can't decide whether or not he feels mollified, whether that's such a good thing. So he retreats to the kitchen, to the calm task of scraping plates and loading the dishwasher. His years as a physical therapist have taught him to take delight in small tasks, the minute increments of progress, as his patients perform the simple recuperative exercises he teaches them. After so many years of chaos, he's happy to indulge this urge. Though their names are still on a phone tree for ACT-UP, he and Jordan no longer get urgent calls summoning them to a zap—a sit-in at an ER that turned away a patient with AIDS or a choreographed heckling at another scientific conference. Their warrior days are over.

When he comes out to clear away the dessert dishes, Lawrence and Jordan are bent over the portfolio again, their heads so close that each time they exhale their breath must pool. Jordan glances up once, and Jim raises his wrist and points at his watch, but Jordan ignores him. It's vital for him to adhere to his drug regimen, but of course he won't take his pills while Lawrence is here. With new people, Jordan is closeted about his HIV-positive status.

Jim listens to the flattery coming out of Jordan's mouth, the cooing and seduction that he'll later dismiss as "just business." But Jim isn't blind. He knows what it means when Lawrence lets his hand linger on Jordan's, when the slender corridor of space between their two bodies narrows.

When they were still running scared, when they didn't know if Jordan would respond to combination therapy, Jim would fill a bubble bath for Jordan every night. Jordan would sink into the tub, and Jim would sponge suds onto Jordan's back, remove an arm from the froth to stroke it, lift a leg and work the sponge in circles until he got as far down Jordan's thigh as the bubbles, pausing at the lighter-than-air barrier of the froth. Then he'd dip the sponge below the surface so deftly that Jordan would arch his back with pleasure, shake with the desire they were so deliciously holding off, so artfully sustaining in the face of all their necessary precautions.

Lawrence says something in a sly voice, and Jordan leans against him. And Jim can't help the spiteful, hausfrau sentiment: After all I've done for you.

Jordan comes home looking feverish, but it's happiness that has flushed his skin. When he kisses Jim, he presses his hips against Jim's insinuatingly.

"You should get out more often," Jim says.

Jordan counts on his fingers the clubs he and their friends visited—the 1100, the Eagle, the Motherlode. "There are still guys who wear chaps," he says gleefully. "But they're fighting a losing battle. All the clubs are going upscale, renovating. Half the people in them now are straight. They're trying to assimilate us."

Jim envies whoever was present to witness Jordan's pleasure tonight. Jordan was supposed to call and leave a message on the answering machine so that Jim could meet up with the gang later, after his volunteer shift at the hospital was over.

But it's not too late for him to take advantage of Jordan's mood. Jim moves back into Jordan's arms, maneuvers him slowly but steadily toward the bedroom, where he carefully laid his seductive trap while he waited for Jordan's call. He set out brandy glasses on the bedside table, put on a jazz CD, lit the fat scented candles on the bureau. He swept the brocade pillows and Kewpie doll from the bed and stuck them in the closet with his other tacky treasures, retired one by one over the last two years.

He tugs Jordan down onto the bed when their knees bang against it, offers him the glass of brandy so handily within reach, and watches him take the tiniest sip. Jim peels off Jordan's shirt with a choreographed boldness. They've been together long enough that trying anything new feels awkward, but Jim has rehearsed his tactics. He oils his hands and begins to massage Jordan's back. Earlier tonight, when he gave massages to the patients on the AIDS ward, he experimented with scented oils and gentler chakra techniques, trying to expand his therapeutic repertoire to include the lascivious.

"You're so good to me," Jordan murmurs.

Sleepily Jordan turns over and reaches up to pull Jim down for a kiss.

"You're not too tired?" Jim says.

Jordan gives Jim a kiss that sets off flares in his veins. Then Jordan pulls away. "Pete and Rory were downing Depth Charges all night. And we're in this dance club, and there's a circle of guys dancing with their pants pulled down around their ankles—don't ask *me* why. And Pete gets it in his head that he's hot tonight, and he goes out on the floor and joins them. Pete! In his plaid boxer shorts."

"You didn't drink like that, did you?" Jim asks.

"I outdid them all," Jordan says. "Pete and Rory had to go home in a cab, and Lawrence and I were the only ones left standing. We went on to Badlands before we called it a night."

"Lawrence was with you?"

"Well, you know, we ran into him at one of the bars. And it was like the good old days—running into people and moving on in a horde to the next place."

Jealousy burns through Jim. He won't let it spoil their evening, interrupt the long, passionate kiss that Jordan gives him. It's been so long since they have had sex that he feels he could come just from being kissed. But is it some halo effect of Lawrence that makes Jordan so responsive?

Jim is sorry that he made a point of doing his duty tonight. And it has become a duty. More and more of the patients on the ward are intravenous drug users, people who don't come in until they're way too sick, who don't hug the volunteers and make kiss noises in the air. The fancy brunches are down to once a month now. Sometimes before he enters a room, Jim has to tell himself, I'm not scared. He gets thrown out of the room by these patients or has to work their wasted muscle tissue in grim silence, at a loss for cheery chat. When they yell at him or complain, he's reminded of the one time he and his mother ever discussed AIDS, a disease she wished to keep as remote from her field of vision as his sexual preference. His mother said that she felt sorry for the innocent victims, the people who got AIDS from blood transfusions. What good is mercy, he thinks, if everyone arrives at some boundary line of exhaustion or indifference?

"It was kind of cool kicking around with Lawrence," Jordan says. "Did you know he's having a one-man show at the Knoedler in New York next fall? He's only twenty-eight. He's a real golden boy."

For Jim there's some comfort in the envy that saturates Jordan's voice.

Jim raises himself on an elbow to stroke Jordan. Jordan squints and blinks, squints and blinks. "What is it?" Jim says.

Jordan laughs. "I really did drink too much. You keep splitting in two when I look at you. Sort of separating out from yourself."

"You're seeing double?" One of the warning signs of CMV is blurred vision. If he and Jordan are alert, they can catch an opportunistic infection like CMV in time to treat it.

Jordan shoves Jim off of him abruptly. "What was really nice about being with Lawrence was that he wasn't monitoring me every minute."

Tears shimmer Jim's own vision. "That's not fair."

"You act like it's your disease too. The pill timer goes off at 5 A.M. for me, but you're the one jumping out of bed to fetch the pills."

"Sometimes you just turn off the beeper and roll right over."

"I just want—I want some goddamn privacy."

Jim rolls away from Jordan. He bunches the sheet in his fist and tears at its seam, shredding the hem, a surreptitious destruction. Jordan remains on his back, rigid, and Jim imagines him pinned beneath the same weight that forces Jim's own fingers to wreak their vengeance on such a small scale.

After a long time Jordan reaches over to touch Jim's shoulder. "I'm sorry."

Their lovemaking is nothing like the wild bash that Jim had planned. But their bodies are only slowed, not halted, by the weight that compresses them. In his head Jim hears Miss Saigon belting out her woes, lamenting all that she's sacrificed for love, only to be abandoned, but his body ignores the soundtrack, shamelessly pursues pleasure. After they make love, Jordan lets Jim fold around him momentarily and then disentangles himself. They lie with their backs to one another, each curled into a tight knot, a closed, hard bud.

They have arranged the beach umbrellas as a windbreak and wrapped themselves in the towels they brought to lie on, all except for Rory, who lies shirtless in the sand, insisting it's warm. Baker Beach, sheltered by the curve of Land's End and closer to the mouth of the bay, is a better bet than Ocean Beach would have been, and the fog has already retreated to unveil the rust-orange span of the Golden Gate Bridge. Still, they have to imagine that the weather at the beach is summer weather. This is what they always have to do, Jim thinks, reimagine foggy San Francisco into tropical California real estate, just as they must struggle to sustain a mirage of whimsy in a world that wants to hurt them.

Only Rory's black lab, Guinevere, dares to go near the water. Pete, Rory, Jordan, and Jim remain huddled together on the sand. Rory extols the virtues of echinacea and valerian to Jordan. Rory believes in former lives and aromatherapy, and Jordan enjoys bedeviling him. "What about people poisoning themselves with L-tryptophan?" Jordan says. "None of this stuff is regulated by the FDA."

"Oh, the good old FDA," Rory says. "We know that they're our friends. You put AZT in your body, but you're afraid to take a little packet of dried flowers."

"I'm sick of running after every new fad," Jordan says. "Searching the Internet every time there's another rumor about a new drug."

Guinevere bounds toward them, and when she halts beside

Rory to shake herself, the rest of them scoot out of her way. But Rory lies unperturbed.

"You'd rather trust the government?" Rory says. "With its excellent track record? You gotta go to the underground. It's the only place where people still tell the truth."

Jordan laughs. "Dream on, Rory. What's next—the conspiracy theory?"

Rory makes a tsk-ing sound. "You've turned out to be so bourgeois. We all have. We don't even go to the nude end of the beach anymore."

"Why bother, now that they've closed the Presidio?" Mournfully, Pete glances up at the cliffs above the beach, studded with cypresses that screen the former barracks of the army base. "It's not as much fun anymore. The soldiers aren't up there with their field binoculars trying to get an eyeful."

From this distance the few lunatics willing to go naked on the beach today look like big pink thumbs.

"Those recruits weren't looking at us anyway," Jim says.

"Hah," Rory says. "Anybody who's that interested in a long, smooth rifle is ripe for the picking. 'Come on *down*, soldier boy.'"

Jordan lolls in the sand. "Rory's right. We're all bourgeois. So fucking careful about everything. The only wanton people I know are the artists I work with. They still have great big hissy fights with their lovers and break dishes when they're mad. Jim, you'd never shatter Lenox in anger, would you?"

"Now who's dreaming?" Jim says. "I've been to one too many openings with you. No one ever talks to me for more than five minutes. There's no gain in it."

"Jim, honey," Pete says. "Forget it. You can't fake cynicism. It has to come from the heart."

Jordan gets to his feet. "I'm going to the other end of the beach." He tugs the windbreaker from his shoulders and knots it around his waist, and then he yanks off his shirt and swim trunks.

"Trying to keep up with Pete's antics the other night?" Rory says. "You're such wild things, you give me the shivers."

Jordan steps over Rory, splattering sand onto him. He stalks off, windmilling his arms to shoo Guinevere when she races after him.

"Why is he so bitchy lately?" Pete says.

Just as he can't help watching Jordan go, Jim can't help wanting to snatch up his clothes and chase him. Jim believes the old wives' tales about how you catch a cold.

When he catches up to Jordan, Jordan marches on without a word, but he can't exactly stride away when he has to keep batting at the flapping windbreaker. His near nakedness here, where his skin is stippled with goose bumps and washed pale by the harsh light that reflects off the sand, has no more allure than the lumpy bodies of the few naked people watching them pass. Panting, Jim struggles to catch up to him again, shove the bunched clothes at him.

Jordan turns to him with a vindictive expression. "God, you're out of shape."

"If it's a beautiful body you want, you can always try Lawrence's gym."

Jordan bats Jim's hand away. "I'm sick of your petty jealousy."

Where did everything go? Jim cannot reach into himself for the certainty of romance, the plunging risk of their first frantic touching, the seamless fit of their bodies in sleep, the many times in clinic waiting rooms when he folded his hands over Jordan's, when he could imagine their joined hands had the impermeable density of a rock.

"What are we doing wrong?" Jim says. "We should be so grateful."

Jordan clenches his fists. "Easy for you to say."

Jim wishes this were just as hard for him. But he does not have to peel back his lips to check his gums for bleeding every morning. Which makes his wish hypothetical. As hypothetical as the readiness of the soldiers who used to fill the barracks above the beach, waiting ingloriously for their war, while in the city the invisible assault of the plague took more men than did all the battles of the century.

"We've got a chance," Jim says. "We can fix up the house now. Maybe put in a garden."

Jordan turns to face the water. "You probably want kids. And then you'll join the PTA and volunteer for bake sales."

Jim and Jordan have never talked about having kids. Jim doesn't even know if an HIV-positive man could qualify to adopt and has never inquired.

"What's so wrong with that?" Jim says.

"I don't know," Jordan says. "Leave me alone!"

That's just what Jim has to do, he sees that now. They've sunk the hooks of their love so fiercely into such a small portion of each other's flesh.

Rory's dog races up to them. She skids to a halt before Jordan, barks, then jumps on him, her nails scoring red slash marks on his bare thighs.

"Go away, Guinevere," Jordan shouts.

Jim bundles Jordan's clothes under one arm and picks up a stick of driftwood. He tosses it for the dog, and she hurtles after it and promptly brings it back. Toss and fetch. Again. Again.

"Look at me," Jordan says. "These wonder drugs redistribute fat from your arms and legs to your back and belly. I'm gonna have a potbelly that sticks out like a goiter. I might as well make hay while the sun shines."

"You slept with him!"

"Can't you imagine anything that isn't a cliché?"

There's a kind of betrayal Jim could stand. The soap opera of Jordan sneaking around on him, yes. But not this. He feels as cold toward himself, toward the pillow-soaking, jealous crying fits he won't have, as he does toward Jordan.

The dog trots back to them, and this time Jordan shoves her away from him.

"Don't start crying," Jordan says.

Jim does not feel a bit like crying.

"Oh, the silent treatment again." Jordan heaves a shuddering sigh. "Why don't you just smother me now? Sacrifice one of your brocade pillows and get it over with."

Guinevere, dripping wet, returns with the stick.

"You pest," Jordan says.

Guinevere takes this as an invitation and leaps for Jordan. By the time they beat her off, Jordan is caked with wet sand.

Jordan scrubs the sand from his forearms with utilitarian haste, when the slope of muscle and sinew there is so beautifully articulated. When Jim reaches out to help him, Jordan holds still, looks away, his cheeks shame-flushed like a child's. The friction of the sand must make the most gentle touch chafe, especially at his elbows, where the skin is bruised, thinned from having blood drawn so often, a tender, near transparent envelope.

Jim hesitates before he brings his hand up along the curve of Jordan's arm. He's afraid now of how easy an embrace could be. What seemed to be a gift withheld turns out to be the hardest thing.

Guinevere noses her way between them, her whole body undulating, her tail whacking their legs, a blunt club of delight.

Jordan laughs. "Can't you leave us in peace?"

Then he yanks the stick from the dog's mouth and arcs it into the air as hard as he can.

light, air, water

When Vince and I lead Elena into the green-
house, she stands still a moment, breathing in the calm. The air
is thick as syrup—a wetness burdened with the acidic odor of the
bark chips in which I pot the plants, the medicinal sharpness of
pesticides, the idiosyncratic perfume of the orchids. Crowded on
benches, the flowers hover on slender stalks, pale or brilliantly
hued creatures poised for flight, their waxy petals flared like out-
spread wings, ruffled like intricate crests, or spurred like the elaborate tails of tropical birds. In this fantastic aviary, the orchids
seem about to shift into life, swoop, soar, alight on brittle legs, but
they remain forever caught in the arrested stillness of their clever
mimicry.

Vince found Elena standing outside the greenhouses crying. I
was waiting in the office for her, and he led her back to me. Instead of interviewing her for the job in the greenhouse, I made her
tea while Vince fetched her a box of Kleenex. She apologizes now
for crying, launches into an unnecessary explanation. She's just
come back from Spain, where she'd flown to join her boyfriend on
a trip through Europe, a trip they'd planned for months, a college
graduation present to themselves. He'd gone ahead of her because

she had to take a last course in summer school. He met her plane with his new woman at his side.

I take Elena through all three greenhouses. When I encourage her to smell a cycnoches—bananas and vanilla—her misery gives way to a pleased absorption that I suspect is her natural state. I work the conversation around to the job I advertised in the local paper. Bolinas is neither city nor country, cut off from the rest of Marin County by long, winding roads and populated by dropouts and artists of various kinds, and I struggle to find people willing to work here part-time.

Elena says she isn't sure how long she'll stay. Her voice wavers. "But I can't live forever on what's left of the traveler's checks I brought back with me."

Behind her back, Vince smiles. It would be hard for Vince or me not to feel a bit nostalgic faced with Elena, red-faced and snotty, so young, so heartbroken, so surprised to have been slapped so hard. Forgetting us, she gnaws at the inflamed skin around her fingernails, yet still she's lovely in her ungainly sadness, with her silky long hair and her pale skin, so pleasing in her barely plump sleekness.

After Elena starts at the greenhouse, Vince begins finding excuses to hang around. We broke up again a few months ago, but he has always had free access. He does carpentry work for me, and my house is on the property, flanked by the garden he still tends, and Nuala always loves to see her father. Drawn by the nectar of Elena's dogged grief, he tries too hard. He comes by just to tell her a joke or give her a bird book, recklessly generous the way he is with eight-year-old Nuala.

Vince makes a living from construction work the same way that I make a living from the greenhouse, deliberately earning just enough. We met when he came to rebuild one of the greenhouses years ago. Early on he established a pattern of leaving, going away on trips of four months or more, so that it became part of the natural flux of things. At other times I would get involved in something else—in Nuala when she was small, in the greenhouse when the business wasn't going well—and not have enough energy left over to give him the kind of attention he wanted. Vince likes his romance but only in bursts. He'll waltz me off to the northern coast for a week, and then I won't see him for a month, though he lives only a few streets away.

So of course Elena's single-mindedness fascinates him, even though he's going to such lengths to break her will. He comes by to pick her up after work, two bikes in the bed of his truck. He shows up with an elaborate springtime bouquet of wildflowers. One morning I catch him stroking the back of her hand when he's supposed to be repairing water pipes. Caught, Vince comes up with an explanation, holds out one of Elena's blunt little paws to show me her scraped knuckles and wonder how she's done that to herself.

I follow him out to his truck when he loads up his tools later in the morning. "She's going to take every little thing seriously," I say.

He leans against the truck with a sly grin on his face, and like a wave of homesickness, a stirring of desire for him comes over me. He's loose-limbed from all these years on construction sites, always tan, and his hair has an appealing unruliness, just like his crooked and self-satisfied smile.

"I don't want her to be a casualty of your midlife crisis," I tell him.

We water by hand in the greenhouses. I can tell by hefting a pot whether a plant needs water, though I am having only erratic success in training Elena to do the same. If the plants have well-established roots, they can survive almost anything you throw at them. Most orchids can grow if you slap them on a piece of wood, seeming to flourish on air alone. They have simple requirements: water, bright indirect light, and a well-aerated potting medium. But it can be tricky to get them to bloom, to recreate artificially the prerequisite of a winter season. When the days shorten, when the dwindling span of light triggers the cryptic code of their flowering, they must be watered less and kept at a cooler temperature. Even then some of them refuse to flower, and I have to switch fertilizers or move them from the temperate greenhouse to the warm greenhouse, trying to guess the reason for their obstinacy.

When Elena and I finish watering, we sort through the plants that have been retrieved that day from clients. I grow my own plants for sale, but the bulk of my business involves boarding orchids for collectors, delivering them to their owners when they bloom, and fetching them back when they've spent their beauty.

Elena hears Vince's truck in the drive before I do, and she pauses in her work, confident that this visit is for her. When he comes into the greenhouse, he kisses me first and then turns to Elena, wrapping his arms around her and kissing her hard. Over his shoulder, she looks at me with alarm.

She is clumsy. She overwaters or breaks off still succulent roots when we're inspecting the plants. It's easy enough to do—the oxygen-hungry roots of orchids typically push up through the bark chips and over the rim of any pot. Yet she plows into her mistakes as if compelled, her eyes widening at what her hands are doing, and then apologizes piteously, her feelings far more delicate than her fingers. I have to console her and promise she's done no harm.

"Can you leave work a little early today?" Vince asks Elena. "I have something I want to show you. But you need a warm coat."

He'll take her out to Kelham Beach in Point Reyes. The sunset is spectacular there on a clear, windy day like this. With Elena, he can watch the sun go down for the first time again, talk her into sleeping on the beach just because they haven't packed supplies, convince himself of the impetuousness of his wooing.

Vince says he has a job to get to, and Elena walks him out, her arm snaking around his waist. She comes back rosy cheeked—been kissed again, further embarrassed by the sheer profusion of Vince's attentions. We work in silence for a while, and then Elena says, "I'm sorry, Jo."

"What for?"

"It's like he made a point of coming here, showing off."

Not Vince, but Elena, with the color rising high in her face, seems compelled to show off. "He's in and out of here all the time," I say. "I don't think he thought twice about it, to tell you the truth. He's got a kid parked here somewhere, after all. And we're friends. We've always been friends."

"Well, I just think it must be hard."

I pinch an aphid from a leaf and crush it between my fingers. "You get over these things," I say.

Elena, at twenty-three, is incapable of recognizing the broad tapestry of the story she's stepped into. With the tunnel vision of lust, she can't see past or around Vince. She can't imagine what it's like to be forty, to have my child's life dependent on mine, to be sated with the passion of that bond, ballasted by the serene and orderly structure of my days in the greenhouse, stuffed full on the bounty of my own kitchen garden and the beauty of this place, privileged to filch an exquisite stalk from a plant in the greenhouses whenever I please.

In my first years here I was taken up with the struggle to pay off the loans I'd cobbled together to buy the land, immersed in rebuilding the greenhouses, installing insulation, benches, a drainage system. Vince came and went, helping me add on to the one-room house. There were other men, and I exercised the freedom to choose my working hours so that I had time for the beach, hiking, the long evenings at home that were essential to any love affair out here. I was making something, my own pleasure, the space in which I could live my life as I pleased.

When I decided I wanted a child, Vince happened to be available and willing, once I assured him that I wouldn't expect him to stay around because of the baby. The romance of Nuala linked us even when other kinds of romance failed us. Vince spent the winter of her sixth year in Thailand and sent her postcards every day—he finds postcards of cats to send her no matter where he is in the world—and he came to dinner the night he came home. I was seeing Bennett then, a field biologist who lived north of town and who was friends with Vince in the way most people who've lived here a long time end up either friends of a kind or enemies. Nuala had learned to read while Vince was away, and after dinner Bennett, Vince, and I sat on the sofa to listen to her, standing with a picture book held open in her hands. By the time she was finished, I found I'd locked my fingers with Vince's, an automatic reorientation and an easy one either to wander into again or to let rest.

Elena helps me wash dishes after dinner while everyone else sits around the cleared table to play poker, Nuala cradled in her father's lap so they can play together. The kitchen still smells of dinner, the tang of balsamic vinegar, the sweet heaviness of garlic and rosemary and roast chicken. Elena clatters dishes in the sink, Susan mutters over her cards, Andrea and Sam exchange lazy comments with Bennett, and Vince refills wine glasses like a good host. Bennett complains about the group of people who last week lay down in front of the bulldozers when the county attempted to cut down a stand of eucalyptus on the road into town.

"They give us tree huggers a bad name," Bennett says. "All this uproar, when eucalyptus are invaders. They're non-native."

"I'm surprised they could find more than three people in Bolinas who could agree to do the same thing at the same time," Andrea says. She sighs. "Sam and I have been trying for years to get the neighbors to fill in the potholes on our road, and nobody will agree to it, not even if we pay for a truckload of gravel ourselves."

The clay roads out here are shaped into craters and hillocks by winter rains, then baked by summer sun till they're swirled like a lava flow. They're hell on the undercarriage of a car. The county doesn't maintain our roads, by mutual consent with the residents, who have a knee-jerk fear of any form of organized authority.

"But why not?" Elena asks. "It's such a simple, practical thing."

Everyone laughs, and only Vince bothers to answer. "The potholes keep outsiders from using the roads. So they'll leave us alone." Bolinas has something of a siege mentality. Stinson Beach, just down the highway, is jammed with tourists and city folk in summer. The county road signs directing traffic from U.S. 1 into Bolinas are routinely torn down as soon as they're put up.

Vince takes his turn as dealer and changes to another deck of cards, a deck he spent the afternoon arranging in order to rig the game so that Nuala would win a huge pot. I have to enjoy Nuala's triumph, so I come to the table, loop an arm over Bennett's shoulder, platonic remnant of our brief affair. Elena comes after me and drifts around the table.

Susan grumbles when Vince insists they raise the ante in this game to fifty cents. When Elena leans down to look at the cards in Susan's hands, Susan folds the cards in her palm. "Look, if you're not playing, could you step back from the table?"

Susan resents having no chance to win this hand, and besides, her lover left her a few years ago for a younger woman, and she is only too ready to be outraged on my behalf. Before we sat down to dinner, she hissed in my ear, "He has no right to bring her here." Her righteousness amuses me; she had a flirtation with Vince herself during one of those periods when he and I were just friends. Elena will suffer if she wants to be possessive: I've shared a lover, somewhere along the line, with most of my women friends, and I've slept with most of the men I know, or they've slept with a woman who's slept with a man I've been with. How else could it be in a small town full of aging hippies?

When she wins the hand, Nuala scoops the mound of coins toward her and then slides out of her father's lap to count them.

Elena takes Nuala's place in Vince's lap.

"Now do we have to let Elena win a hand?" Susan says.

"Susan," Sam scolds. "You need another drink."

Elena yawns and curls against Vince's shoulder, her hands fluttering across his chest. Her poor little hands—in addition to the raw mess she's made of the skin around her fingernails, she's slashed her fingers and knuckles working in the greenhouses. But she won't wear gloves.

Vince flicks one of her hands out of his way so he can throw a few more quarters into the pot. "Come on, honey, I'm trying to play cards."

Nuala sidles up beside her father and says to Elena, "That's *my* lap."

Vince grins and cocks an eyebrow at Elena.

"OK," Elena says, rising to her feet. "I get the message."

"Oh God," Vince says. "I'm getting too old for this."

Elena turns her back on him, reaches the door in three steps, and slams it behind her on the way out.

Vince bows his head as if he has to hide the grin that lingers on his face. But then he chugs the last of his wine, hugs Nuala, thanks me for dinner, and rushes after Elena. His boots clatter on the porch, and then we hear the blur of beseeching words with which Elena deluges him when he catches up to her in the yard.

I could not be so easy about the promiscuity of my twenties if not for the decade I spent with Vince, a decade in which the easy attachment I felt for him revised what had come before, enabled me to see myself as living loosely by intention, not by accident, a woman who did not depend on men for much even when she enjoyed them.

We split up when I was pregnant with Nuala because Vince fell for a woman from New York who was backpacking through California. He went to New York with her for a couple of months and then came back alone. He wanted to talk to me about her — she'd been rigid and difficult, and things had ended badly between them. We took long walks on the beach nearly every afternoon, and soon enough his confessions led to our holding hands, kissing, exploring the mechanics of accommodating my big belly when we made love.

We were walking at Abbott's Lagoon up in the Point Reyes headlands when Vince asked me if I wanted him to be with me when I gave birth. The lagoon was thick with birds, but aside from their cries it was quiet enough that we could hear the surf pounding just beyond the sandbar that shaped the lagoon, hear the hollow thwack of the pelicans beating their wings against the water, like the clapping of erasers.

"Do you want to be with me?" I said.

I'd become practiced at answering Vince's questions with questions. It was our way of flirting. He'd been away for most of the pregnancy, and it seemed the season for needing him had passed. Every now and then, I'd get irritated that we hardly ever spent the night at his house, that when we did I'd have to forage for a towel or clear a space for my clothes. He'd built onto the original shack in piecemeal fashion, not like a contractor but like some kind of pack rat, adding nooks and crannies or a sleeping loft when the house became overstuffed, till the place was a maze of rooms, jammed with old bicycle tires, car parts he might someday find a use for, seven years of back issues of *The New Yorker* stacked against the wall of the loft. There was hardly room for him to move in it, much less another person.

"I could get a beeper, so you could reach me," Vince said.

"If you had a beeper I might start calling you five or six times a day, like your New York woman."

"She just about drove me crazy," he said. "Every conversation turned into an interrogation. She reminded me of my mother."

I didn't even know his mother's name. His father, he let slip once, had been a lawyer. Vince had a degree from some college back East, but I didn't know which one. He was a determined dropout, never taking contracting jobs that promised big headaches and big profits. My brothers had loaned me money to help me start the greenhouse, my mother was already sending me crocheted blankets for the baby, but Vince lived as if he had entered the world all alone. Just because he never spoke of his family, I imagined them as rich, cold, aristocratic.

Snowy plovers, fat as chickadees, and narrow-breasted dowitchers rose into the air with aggrieved cries as we approached them along the shore of the lagoon. I wondered if the pelicans clustered in the water would scatter at our approach too, if in a flock of hundreds they could be scared off by just two intruders. I ran at the water before Vince could stop me, as awkward as the big heavy birds that swerved away from us as one, beating their wings against the water, rising into the air, and then wheeling to land a little farther out in the lagoon.

Vince kept walking, head down, as if to make a point of dissociating himself from my rude trespass.

"How come your mother's never come out here for a visit?" I said. "Is she sick or something?"

"You're awfully curious all of a sudden."

"Maybe I should know a little of your medical history, for the baby's sake."

"She has Alzheimer's," Vince said. "She's in a nursing home."

"That's it?" I said. "You're so fucking grudging."

I thought about running at the birds again, repeating that momentary thrill of power when I drove them to flight. But I already knew how they'd react. If I asked Vince to get a beeper, he would, but then he would put it down somewhere, and like any foreign object in the organic chaos of his rooms, it would be repelled, expunged.

Which is why it surprises me to learn that Elena has moved into his house.

When I go to fetch Nuala from the greenhouse so she can start her homework, I find her playing with Elena. Elena is inserting a toothpick into a catasetum, prodding the club-shaped column that pokes up from the heart of the flower. Orchids have such simple, elegant geometry: just three petals and three sepals, always with one petal, the labellum, larger or more ornate than the others, a lascivious mouth beckoning an insect to the nectar guarded by the column.

When Elena presses on the pollen cap at the tip of the column, it spits out a sticky, yellow clump of pollinia, startling Nuala, who laughs with delight. A bug backing out of a flower would be forced to press on that hinged pollen cap, with the same effect. Simple but devious. Of course it would have to be the right bug—each species of the finicky orchid is constructed so that only one kind of bee or moth can pollinate it.

Elena and Nuala jump when I announce myself. "Fooling around on the job again?"

"Mom, you've got to see this," Nuala says.

"It's my trick," I say. "I showed Elena."

Elena transfers the pollen to another flower and promises Nuala that when the flower grows a pollen tube down the stem, they'll plant the seeds. I'm surprised at her inaccuracy, because she's trained in science. It can take three months or longer before the seedpod bursts, spilling grains as fine as face powder. Those tiny seeds, lacking endosperm, can germinate only if they're invaded by a specific fungus. I'd have to send the seeds to the lab in Santa Barbara and wait a year to get plants back. Orchid pollination leaves so much to chance that it's amazing the plants reproduce at all.

"Nuala was a real help," Elena says. "We finished all the repotting."

"But she cut her hand real bad," Nuala says.

"No, I didn't," Elena says.

"Let me see," I say.

Elena reluctantly holds out her right hand. Already a scab is forming over this newest scratch, which crisscrosses older ones, oddly neat, straight scars.

"You should have washed this out," I say. "It's real easy for a greenhouse cut to get infected."

"Oh, I don't care," Elena says in a blurry voice.

I've come to expect this sudden shift into another key, but Nuala is puzzled. "You don't want an infection," she says.

"We had an awful fight," Elena says.

"Mom, is she talking about my dad?" Nuala says.

"Go start your homework," I say.

"Mom," Nuala says. "You never let me stay for the good parts."

"Go." I push her shoulder, but she only gives way when Elena's face puckers.

Once Nuala has gone, I tell Elena, "You're having too many accidents."

"I bought him a shirt," Elena says. "A plain blue dress shirt. You'd think I bought him a straitjacket or something. We were screaming at each other."

Vince doesn't scream. He turns silent and separate when he's mad, is humiliatingly indifferent to the plea of touch.

"He's middle-aged," I say. "He's not interested in changing."

"He's so selfish. He just assumes I'm going to fit right into all his ways, all his habits. I told him to stop acting like a fussy old biddy. We both said terrible things. He said he wasn't going to let me *ride* him."

Elena stares at her hands, the unreadable pattern of cross-hatched slashes. She starts to cry. "That bastard! He had the nerve to encourage me to apply to grad school. 'Go wherever you want.'"

Elena seems to have led such a pleasant life up until the day that boy dumped her. Somewhere, on the peninsula south of San Francisco, she has two parents and a brother and a sister, a home where her school portraits still adorn the wall and her mother has saved her school essays in a box. She met her boy, Jeremy, at Cornell, where they were both placid, excellent biology majors. They were to have spent the year in Europe before going on to graduate school together.

Elena and her mother were already planning her wedding when she left to join Jeremy. From what Elena tells me, she and her mother are close, and maybe this tenderness made it impossible for Elena to go home after she'd been betrayed. If Jeremy had had the good manners to write to her from Spain when he discovered his new true love, she might be in graduate school now, disappointed but resilient, spending her days in the company of young men who'd watch for her shy smile, coax her out of herself again. If Vince had been traveling when Elena first came here, she might never have met him before she moved on. Her father and Vince must be roughly the same age. I can't imagine Vince invited home to dinner with the family, enjoying a drink with the insurance-executive papa in his polo shirt. Elena's mother wouldn't have any illusions about selecting flower arrangements, not when Vince showed up in his paint-spattered shoes and his jeans worn to gray at the knees. How worried Elena's parents would be about her reaction to her heartbreak, how uncertain that the scales would right themselves again in time to save her from her defiant, clumsy efforts to defy nature.

Vince was supposed to come over last night to help Nuala build a model of a log cabin for a school project, but he forgot. Tonight, belatedly, he has remembered, and he shows up at our door, his arms laden with tools and supplies. But Nuala's not ready to forgive him. She'll never get it done now; he never does things when he says he'll do them.

"I'm doing something else instead," Nuala says.

I love Nuala's absolute little heart, but it causes all kinds of difficulties for her. She's bereft whenever Vince forgets a promise or shows up late, cannot forgive his casual notions of responsibility, not even when he compensates generously.

"You've got time to get started now," I tell Nuala.

"He didn't even apologize!" Nuala says.

"Your dad didn't mean to hurt your feelings," I say.

"We don't need a translator," Vince says. "Come on, Nuala, I'm tired."

"Why don't you just go home?" Nuala says. "Go home to your girlfriend!"

"OK." Vince gets up from the table. "I'll come back when you're ready."

Nuala screams when he goes to the door, and Vince flinches in mock horror, then steps out and shuts the door quietly behind him.

Nuala starts to cry. "He doesn't care. He doesn't care!"

I go out after Vince, and he turns to face me.

"Can't you work this out with her?" I say. "I'll never get her to bed tonight."

"Let me have my own relationship with her, will you?"

"Sure. When I'm not the one who gets stuck holding the bag."

"Is there something weird going on with the moon?" Vince says.

"Every female on planet Earth wants a piece of me these days. What the hell did I do?"

"You're just an innocent bystander. Jesus, you don't even see what you're doing to Elena."

"You don't know the first thing," Vince says.

It takes me hours to get Nuala to bed after her father leaves, and then I find that Vince has left his car keys on the table. I don't want him waking us both up at six in the morning when he comes looking for them. I grab a jacket and a flashlight and head down the road to his house.

I almost don't need the flashlight—I have memorized the zig-zag route from my house to his, know my progress by the thicket of blackberries that scratches me as I take a corner, the eerie jutting of a crooked fence into the brief illumination of the flashlight, the dog that bays at a house halfway between his and mine.

Music pours from his house. Miles Davis, *Sketches of Spain*. The big uncurtained windows along the front of the house spill light like drifting smoke into the night. Elena, dressed in a T-shirt of Vince's and underpants, moves before a window, and then Vince comes into view. He's naked, but the sight is so familiar to me—the way his dark chest hair is patterned in rippling Vs like a brace of arrows aimed at the frothy hair of his crotch—that I don't feel startled. He lunges for Elena, who lifts her shirt to expose her breasts before darting into darkness, disappearing, and then reappearing at another window. It's as if I've entered a movie theater halfway through a film in a foreign language: I'm caught, held by the flickering images that I cannot understand, straining to intuit some narrative from the dialogue of their bodies, the chain reaction of their gestures, the unconscious tension of muscles fluidly shaping and reshaping their mouths and eyebrows.

They disappear and reappear again in my field of vision. Elena carries a towel, a steaming bowl of water, a razor. Vince sits on the sofa, and she sits in his lap, facing him, her legs wrapped around his hips. She lathers shaving gel in her hands and slowly smooths it onto his face, caressing the skin, working the flesh to reshape his features. She dips the razor in the bowl of hot water and carefully tracks it across his cheek. Her hand moves slowly, cuts a clean swath through the foam. He kisses her, smearing her face with the white cream. I see her laugh rather than hear it, the sharp, scythed tracks of the muscles around her mouth. I know they can't see me. Even if they were to look in my direction, they'd see only their own reflection against the silvery mirror that night makes of the window.

Elena works beside me at the repotting table, a row of uprooted vandas laid out before her on sheets of newsprint, their fat white roots clawing the air like gnarled, arthritic fingers. Her hands encased in vinyl gloves at my insistence, she trims brown leaves and dead roots before popping a plant into a new pot and shoveling in bark chips.

She starts to clip the next plant, and I remind her sharply to use the propane torch on the shears. She forgets how easy it is to transmit a virus from one plant to another. We have to use the gloves, lay down fresh sheets of newsprint between batches of plants, soak our pots in disinfectant before reusing them.

Vince comes in as she is sterilizing the shears, and she turns to face him with the torch held like a weapon in her hands. "Forget you, mister!"

"Can't you see that I'm trying to think of you?" Vince says. "Can't you give me any credit at all?"

"Will you both *please* do this somewhere else?" I say.

"You don't have to torture me," Vince says. "When you didn't come home last night, I was imagining all kinds of things—"

"You deserve to suffer," Elena says.

She reaches into a bin of bark chips and hurls a handful at him. Vince ducks, then rushes forward to plunge his own hands into the bin. They fling bark chips at each other, making a mess of the floor and the repotting table. I'm tired of them both—their sacrilegious shrieks in the hum of the greenhouse, their utter disregard for my privacy or their own, their recklessness in this place that's a chapel of order and slow, slow time. I don't bother to protest but strip off my gloves and leave them.

Vince finds me in my kitchen having my late night cup of tea. I offer him a cup, but he shakes his head and stands on the threshold as if he's afraid to come in.

"Is Elena here?" he asks.

"Look, you've got to stop conducting your love life on my premises."

"She stormed out on me last night. She takes things wrong. I want her to go to graduate school. I'm trying not to be selfish—I don't want to hold her back. I'm tied down here because of Nuala."

"I'm thrilled you remember her."

"Well, I am a minor shareholder," Vince says. "Shit. I was a prick to start this up with Elena in the first place. I'm too fucking old and set in my ways."

Where I used to dread their painful ending—for Elena's sake—now I just wish they would stop rehearsing it. "You've turned her into my most useless employee, and that's saying a lot. She didn't even show up for work today."

He says, "Please. Help me look for her. The last time she walked out she told me she spent the night in one of your greenhouses. She has nowhere else to go."

We find her in the cool greenhouse where I keep the cymbidiums. As if insulated by the scented hush, she doesn't realize we've come in. She sits on the floor, her back against a bench, knees bent. She's leaning over her left arm, a razor in her right hand, her lower lip caught between her teeth, absorbed in what she's doing: flaying the sleekness of her arm with calm precision, forcing herself past the instinct to hesitate. A neat seam of blood wells in the track of the razor.

Vince freezes, but some maternal instinct, some compound of fury and fear, propels me to Elena, and I slap the razor from her hand.

Vince chokes out, "You need a doctor."

He's standing far enough back that Elena has to search for him when she lifts her head. But her gaze is steady when she finds him. "A head doctor, you mean."

She seems, oh, not vulnerable at all, but hard and stubborn and determined. Still, I cup her hand gently when I bend to inspect the shallow cuts on her arm.

"It doesn't hurt that much," she says.

Her meek voice is such unarguable proof that she belongs to another realm, where her scratches and bruises are ordinary accident, as inconsequential as the clumsiness I've pitied in her and the apologies that trail after it. Some mistake has landed her here with the two of us.

Vince steps closer to Elena and crouches, keeping himself an arm's length from her. The way he shakes his head reminds me of how he shakes his head over a bad piece of carpentry, woeful and condemning all at once. "Jesus Christ, what a mess."

I think we need to bandage her arm before we take her to the hospital, but I have to explain this simple decision twice to Vince before he'll let me go to the office for the first-aid kit. I find it on the shelf, just where it should be. I've never used the first-aid kit, but I feel stupidly confident once I have the little metal box in my hand.

When I come back into the greenhouse, Vince has adopted a pose of solicitude, looped an arm around Elena's shoulder. She jerks against his arm, some muscle spasm, and then he kisses her forehead, her temple, her cheek, tracing a faint tenderness onto her skin.

"I don't want you to be hurt, that's why," Vince murmurs to Elena. "I only want what's best for you."

"I know, I know." Elena is crying again.

The metal box slips from my hand, crashes to the floor, and pops open, spilling its contents. When I kneel to replace the packets of gauze and tubes of ointment in the box, Vince tells me just to grab a few things and bring them, for God's sake.

He has never spoken so urgently to me.

"Shut up," I say. I'm pleased to deny him. I want to see him damaged, burdened. He deserves it.

But in the end I obey him, will my hands to behave. He holds out Elena's arm so that I can squeeze antibiotic ointment onto her wounds. His hands shake so much that I lay down squiggly transparent worms of the gel. I'm afraid to touch her raw skin, too much in the habit of rough competence with the orchids, whose beauty does not require reverence or delicacy.

I wrap Elena's arm like a mummy's, tear the tail end of the gauze into two strips so I can tie it to itself, making a lumpy, loosely spooling package of her arm.

Vince laughs. "Is that really the best you can do?"

Misery makes his voice harsh. And again I'm pleased. I can't tell if this pleasure is vindictive or born of some sympathy I can't help, not after all these years we've known each other.

Elena reaches for me so I can help her to her feet. Her hands transmit to me the raking consciousness of what it means to feel ravaged, broken by one's own will, and in this trembling contact telegraph the slashing force of need.

side by side

Wonder is not what Bill should feel after a truck smashes into his car at forty miles an hour, but he does. He is amazed that he could step unscathed from his crumpled Toyota, amazed by the way his body absorbed the impact. The stack of bones in his spine jumped, scattered, and then resettled, as if his bones had been momentarily freed from their tethers of muscle and tendon and ligament.

Everyone, even the paramedics who came to the scene of the accident and assured Bill he would be in pain tomorrow, seemed as amazed as Bill. You escaped with your life, said the cop who made the report, both of the paramedics, the shaken driver of the truck.

Even Bill's wife, Pam, says so when he comes home to tell her what happened. He finds her in the backyard, barbecuing even though the fog is rolling in, visible as exhaled breath in the cold air. Their old house didn't have a yard, only a rectangle of concrete patio, but here they have a lawn, flagstones, a flower bed. The grass is already jeweled with beads of condensed water. Bill has an impulse he's never had before. He takes off his shoes and socks to cross the lawn to Pam. His feet sink in the damp grass, so cold. With his two hands he mimes for Pam the collapse of his car and watches her face shift, like another kind of mime, from nonchalance to concern to fear. She puts both her hands on his cheeks. They've come through a bad patch recently, and it's good to see that inside his wife, this is what was waiting for him.

She wants him to go to the emergency room right away, and when he refuses, she wants him to lie down. But he feels good. Woozy and only slightly achy in his joints and completely let off the hook, the way he feels when he is coming down with the flu. Bill walks away from Pam and drifts across the wet grass. He imagines his feet leaving a slick snail's trail on the wet lawn. Delicious cold pricks at his toes. He watches the pine tree at the back of the yard shiver a little in the wind and he waits. He has a beatific moment coming to him.

The closest he ever comes to that clarity is when he takes the Vicodin his doctor prescribed for back pain. Throw in the daily dose of muscle relaxants, and Bill can feel mighty fine indeed. Maybe the recognition of having been spared comes grain by grain, like some sort of time-release medication. Maybe he is just distracted by all the trivial ways in which, it turns out, he hasn't been spared. The morning after the accident, Bill decided to call the doctor and discovered he couldn't lift the phone book. His doctor said he had whiplash and he could only expect his pain to grow worse. When Bill called the truck driver's insurance company to file a medical claim, an agent informed him that the truck driver—that man who'd had tears in his eyes when he saw Bill climb out of his car—was claiming the accident had been Bill's fault. Every day, Bill, lying on the sofa with ice packs strapped to his lower back and neck, has to field calls from the bullying substitute who has been taking his high school English classes until he gets back on his feet.

How thin relief seems compared to the leaden compactness of pain. It doesn't keep Bill from being bored with watching TV all week. Sick of Oprah, he wonders how he might find a witness to vindicate him. There must be plenty of them, maybe even someone he knows—the accident happened at rush hour just a few blocks from home. He takes a poster board his son used for a science project and writes a plea for help in large block letters on the back, and at 4:45 he walks to the intersection. He wears the poster like a sandwich board, held in place by twine looped around his neck. Even fortified with Vicodin, he can't stand the strain of holding up the sign with his hands.

Standing on the corner, inhaling the sweet fumes of car exhaust, Bill is encouraged by the fact that so many cars go by. Hundreds every minute. Someone in one of these cars will know what happened to him.

When a van pulls up next to the curb and honks, he is disappointed to discover that the driver is his wife. Pam leans over to unlatch the passenger door for him. "Get in," she says. "Hurry up. Before one of the neighbors sees you."

Bill climbs into the car—slowly, fine-tuned to the compromised functioning of his body. From the back seat, his kids stare. Pam has to pick them up from the after-school program now that Bill can't bring them home with him after school. This has been rotten for her. Ordinarily Bill fetches the kids and does the little daily errands, the late-night run to the grocery when they're out of milk, the kids' dentist appointments, the dry cleaning.

Bill rolls up the poster board and holds it between his knees. "I thought it was worth a shot," he says. "Too many good drugs, I guess."

He's sure Pam will tell him he's crazy, right in front of the kids.

"Let the insurance company handle it," she says.

When they pull into the garage, Pam jumps out of the car to unload groceries from the back, where the bags have been shoved in among the accessories she carts around for the houses she stages. With the bare minimum, Pam can furnish an empty house from her inventory or repair the bad taste of sellers who don't know how to arrange their possessions in a cunning way. People don't just sell a house in San Francisco anymore, not in a market pitched to frenzied desire. Spending a few thousand dollars on Pam's fee and a coat of paint and artful flower arrangements translates into tens of thousands in the actual offer, more like a miracle than an investment.

Pam issues instructions while the kids are still slamming the car doors shut. Arianne is to go and empty the hamper into the laundry basket so Pam can get a wash in, Liam has to set the table, and Bill needs to help them start their homework. Juggling two grocery bags and her purse, Pam frees a hand to grab the mail and uses her elbow to switch on the light on the stairs.

Bill lies down on the sofa to ice his back and tells the kids they have to bring their homework to him. Arianne wants to know why he can't come to her room to help her with long division. She stabs her sheet of notebook paper with her pencil. "See? I can't do it in my lap. It won't work." She begins to weep. "And I can't find my right pencil."

She insists on using only a pastel mechanical pencil for homework. She clips her hair into a ponytail with an elastic hair band that must be new every day, cried this morning because Pam hadn't done a wash, and the shirt she always wore with her corduroy pants was still in the hamper. She can't bear to lose things and accuses her little brother of stealing them when they go missing. Her sneakers must be wiped clean every night or she won't wear them in the morning. She's ten. How can she have so many requirements?

Bill promises to buy more mechanical pencils tomorrow.

"No you won't," Arianne says. "You won't even drive."

These tiny probes of hers uncover such large flaws.

"I can't," Bill says. "Not with my back."

"You don't look like it hurts," Liam says.

Through the soft haze of the drugs, Bill reaches for Arianne. His hand cups her skull, bumpy, somehow stubborn beneath his fingers. She nudges his hand away with the pencil. Liam asks Bill what he should do for his book report. How blank and erasable their faces are, how much like any other kid's face, lips and nose still smudgeable and cheeks smooth and eyes another kind of indefinite. Not written on yet. How large would Bill have had to make the letters on his sign so that they could be read by people in moving cars?

Bill is tired from doing nothing all day. He keeps his eyes half closed even when Liam punches his arm. His children swim like tadpoles in his dimmed and narrowed field of vision. They bicker with one another, a persistent butting of dissatisfaction. Tadpoles. Balls of blind guts with a tail for motility. Pam hollers from the kitchen that Bill could at least keep the kids out of each other's hair. Sounds are as buffered as the pain signals arriving like huffing, smoking locomotives in Bill's brain.

Bill flips through a magazine while Pam conducts business on the cell phone, rearranging the appointments she had to cancel so she could bring Bill here to the back clinic. He can't drive yet. He made a stab at going back to work; he spent one day in his classroom, talking to his students about *Huck Finn,* and whether he stood or sat, any single position made his back hurt. He was up and down and up and down until the accumulated pain at day's end made him wish he could hang himself from a hook.

They didn't expect this would take all morning. The specialist examined Bill in less than fifteen minutes, but the X ray he sent Bill for required an hour's wait, and now they are waiting again for the specialist to interpret the results. When Bill stood in the dark X-ray room, holding his breath while the technician took the picture, he had a moment when he thought he might faint. He felt queasy, as if the injury had been inflicted fresh, first by the doctor's hands during the exam — mere touch inflaming every nerve in his back — and then by the technician's hands as he positioned Bill before the plate that held the film.

Bill watches Pam punch out numbers on the phone, demolishing her list of calls, brisk and chatty. She smiles as if the person on the other end of the line can see her, keeps trying to tuck a loose strand of blond hair back into her ponytail, smoothing her hair in place, this quiet gesture betraying her anxiety only to him, like a private gift of love. His wife. His sweetie.

What was that bad patch about anyway? Irrelevant stuff. Bickering over Bill failing to put up the screens on the windows or not talking to Pam the right way about things. So what? What did they even have to discuss? Whether Liam needed to be tested for learning disabilities because he didn't like to read, Arianne should be coaxed to make more friends, or Bill should think about moving into administration. Whether Bill complained that Pam had missed the school play and most of Liam's soccer games because he resented her for being the big breadwinner.

Is that all it was about? The housing market in San Francisco has cooled a bit, but when it was peaking, Pam worked like crazy; everyone in real estate was scrambling to make a buck before the bubble burst. The houses Pam staged sold for 8 percent more than comparable ones. She kept her cell phone on the table when they had dinner; in real estate you worked the hours when clients were at leisure to tour houses. She adopted the habits of the realtors who supplied her with clients; she wore a lot of perfume, bought handbags that matched her shoes, indulged in a lavish gift exchange with the realtors. They sent Pam wine-and-fruit baskets when a sale closed, and she boxed for them leather desk sets and raku bowls. In the worst of the frenzy, Bill, not Pam, woke up sweating in the middle of the night, began talking in his sleep. Loud enough that Pam would have to elbow him to shut him up.

Bill stands up to relieve his back. Pam looks at him. "Does it hurt?"

He has to take a breath before he answers. "I just got this weird stabbing pain. Usually it's a dull ache, this dense sensation."

Pam laughs. "Dense sensation? This isn't English class. You don't have to interpret it."

Bill laughs with her. "I'm beginning to understand how hypo-chondriacs get the way they are."

"The back X ray will turn out to be a waste of time," Pam says. "You should push this doctor for an MRI."

Another insult to his precious pain. Bill's doctor was reluctant to refer him to this specialist and noncommittal about whether seeing a chiropractor would help. Walk, the doctor said. Walk for forty minutes a day. Now the specialist seems convinced Bill's pain stems from nothing but tendon and muscle damage. He autho-rized the X ray only because Bill asked for it.

"What if I insist on an MRI for nothing?" Bill says. "This is my manhood at stake here, honey."

Bill can't tell if the walking is doing him much good. He goes out in the neighborhood at dusk and walks streets he has only ever driven through. Their new neighborhood has stucco houses with tiled roofs and soothing green lawns, a far cry from their old neighborhood of ticky-tacky boxes built in the sixties. Bill savors the flower beds, the trees, the flagstone paths, and wrought iron fences of this neighborhood, all the ornamentation that evinces a careful husbandry. He feels sorry that he teased Pam when month after month last spring they spent their Sundays hunting for just the right house. On his walks he has scouted a couple of houses for her, come home to announce For Sale signs on lawns, and she's about to sign a contract for one of them, a house left empty by its former tenants. Now he takes a proprietary interest in that house, in all the houses whose gardens and window treatments he has memorized in his slow pacing. The lit windows, tantalizing behind drawn curtains, beckon him, and on those rare occasions when he passes an uncurtained window, he slows to seize this glimpse through a peephole into another world.

A nurse opens the door to the inner office and calls Bill's name. The back specialist doesn't smile when Bill enters his office, and Bill immediately begins to sweat. He knows too many people who've had back surgery and were the worse for it. Or who went from specialist to specialist until finally and too late someone discovered the damage.

The back specialist clips Bill's X ray to a light board. Bill can read nothing in the swirly grays that make his solid skeleton look as if it were made of smoke.

"There's mild joint damage," the doctor says, tapping the X ray. "But that could be arthritis. A simple fact of your age. It proves nothing."

What can Bill say? *I demand an* MRI *for my dense sensation!*

When Bill comes out to the waiting room after just a few minutes, Pam looks up expectantly. He's ashamed he has so little to report to her.

Bill shrugs. "Whiplash doesn't show up on an X ray."

She smiles. "But that's good news."

"How can it hurt like this, and nothing shows up?"

"Get that MRI," Pam says. "So you can put this behind you."

When she stages houses, Pam does simple things like remove ruffled valances from curtain rods, set out a wine rack on a kitchen counter, move sofas and chairs in from the walls, set out towels of a certain delicious color in the bathroom, replace a spider fern with a blooming phalaenopsis. Pam can predict what triggers wanting, and it's so simple, nothing complicated about it, nothing hidden from sight.

Bill nags the kids to make lunch for school the next day. He has to stand over them every night to make them do it because they can't manage it in the morning. Five nights a week, nine months of the year, minus four weeks vacation—that's one hundred and sixty times annually. When he made dinner earlier—forcing himself, because it hurt and Pam couldn't be expected to carry him forever—he wondered how many times a day he checked his pocket for keys, calculated how many leaves of lettuce he washed every night, how many dinners—assuming they had dinner out an average of once a week—he would have to make in this decade and the next and the next. Maybe when Bill's bones jumped and scattered and snapped back into place, they landed wrong. Maybe a disk presses on some secret nerve or occludes the flow of blood to his brain.

While Pam finishes the day's calls, Bill stands over Liam and Arianne to make sure they brush their teeth, which they should do for a full 2 minutes, or 728 minutes a year, and as he kisses them good night and tucks them in, he totals the number of bedtime kisses he has given them so far in their lives. Thousands.

Pam comes into the living room after she delivers her kisses to the kids. She twirls. "Free at last," she says, which she says nearly every night after they get the kids into bed. She sits on Bill's lap, facing him, straddling his legs.

He's a little surprised. He thought she might be mad at him. He has refused to get an MRI, couldn't come up with a better reason than embarrassment. Pam will shrug off clients who insist on leaving their bowling trophies on the mantel, and she has apparently cut her losses with him too.

Pam unbuttons his shirt. "Now let's have sex."

There's something about her bluntness. It's good for him.

Pam kisses him and slips her hands under his shirt. Then she gets up and leaves him. She has gone to brush her teeth and get ready for bed. Like a commercial break. They'll meet in the bedroom and take up again as if there were no interruption.

While she's in the bathroom, Bill strips off his clothes and gets under the covers, shy. This is the first time.

Pam talks to him while she undresses. She hangs up each garment as she removes it, snapping out wrinkles. In bra and underpants she removes her jewelry and her watch. The chunky metal links of her watch make Bill think of her heavy key ring, the one she drops in the bowl by the front door when she comes home, carefully tagged keys to all the houses to which she has access. Keys. Checking for his keys in his pockets, two dozen times a day. Fingering the key he lifted from Pam's key chain yesterday, stroking it in his pocket while he took his daily stroll.

She crawls into bed with him. "I did three houses today, way too many. It's so hard to turn down work right now. Everybody's holding their breath, waiting for the market to slack off. Be glad you don't have the stress I do at work."

No. Now that he's back at school, the only pressure he gets is from students who want to know when he'll hand back the last papers they turned in. Sixteen hundred pages per class per semester. Yesterday, for maybe the thirtieth time in his life, Bill talked to his students about the river and the shore in *Huck Finn*. He was saying something about the river, the fluid freedom of natural man, the search for meaning, when he felt a sharp pain in his back, pain like a directional arrow instead of the usual seeping ache. It made him think that there was something he could do—something he had to do—to relieve it. Like hunger, it condensed his attention to meeting a single demand. He was in the middle of a sentence. Something about Huck's journey to find meaning. "Find meaning," he said. But he was listening to that other demand. "Find meaning . . . in the meaningful." And all the rest of the day, he felt a craving he could compare only to hunger. A craving he could plan for without being sure that this was what he was doing. When he slipped the key into his pocket, he didn't know that he would use it; he didn't know if it was of any use in staving off this sensation.

Pam kneads Bill's trapezius muscles. "I've been wondering if I should try something else," Bill says.

"What do you mean? Go into administration?"

Pam's touch confuses him. Too light. He's gotten used to the chiropractor, who seems bent on remolding his flesh with her hands. She was interested in the types of his pain. She had him fill in a diagram of his torso, locating every emanating source of hurt in red ink. Then she sank her fingers right into the core of every glowing ember, an artist.

Bill traces figure eights on Pam's arm until she shivers. He says, "Really something else. Something entirely different."

Pam kisses him, tugs his chest hair in smooth circling motions. They're married people all right. They don't bother to demarcate sex from the chitchat that ends their day. She says, "A year ago I'd have told you, get a real estate license. We'll go into business together and make a killing."

"I wouldn't like all those forms you have to deal with when you sell a house," Bill says. "But I don't know what I could try. You're good at figuring out what people want. What do you think I should do?"

Pam moves her hand down to his belly. "I never know too specifically. That's the whole point. If people are still living in the house, we make them take down the family pictures, anything that makes the house seem as if it belongs to someone else. The trick is to give the buyers room to imagine themselves in the house. You set out place mats and pretty dishes and wine glasses and the buyer is like, yeah, if I lived here, I'd have wine with lunch every day. They can see *their* life, only nicer."

It doesn't make any sense to Bill that he wanted to go inside that empty house, that he wants to again. Really he wants to go into all the other houses he walks past. In neighborhoods like theirs, people always draw the curtains so you can't look in, as if to shield the inner sanctum of all that visible cherishing and flaunting. He had to get in somewhere.

It was just an empty house. Pam had not yet transformed it with her props. Sometimes she borrows things from their own house, filches a Moroccan pitcher or a framed watercolor that proves essential to achieving the desired effect.

Pam fishes in Bill's crotch. "Do you enjoy your work?" he says.

Pam giggles. "Which work? What I'm doing now?" Her efforts are producing instant results. "Yeah, I enjoy my work. I'm good at it. That's always gratifying."

Bill's hands scout the solid surface of her. "Is this gratifying?"

He smells her perfume. He wonders how many dabs are in a bottle, how many days of smelling like jasmine. Sometimes when he wakes at night he feels as if the air in the room has thickened with this scent while they sleep. An odor so strong it drowns the smells of the body.

When he enters her, he feels pain spread like warmth across his lower back, like a large hand pressing on his hips from behind. That pain plants itself behind every thrust of his body, and Pam braces him with her hips from beneath. Slap, slap, slap, his hips against hers. A metronome beats out the time, the steady pace of his strokes. Every human on earth must do this to the same rhythm.

"Pammy?" he calls.

Slap, slap, slap, steady and unending as the sound of the ocean.

Bill retrieves his kids from school in a rental car. The kids climb in, banging backpacks and slapping their rumps on the seat and slamming their elbows in that way that kids need to smack you with their physical existence.

"How come you're driving?" Liam says.

Bill shrugs. "I usually do," he says.

It's time. Pam is right about this. If he can do nothing more about his back, he just has to pick up where he left off. It takes only forty minutes, total, to make the circuit from his school to the kids' and then home.

Arianne fidgets, her legs making slick sounds on the vinyl of the car seat. "You forgot to sign my permission slip," she says.

"What permission slip?"

"I gave it to you yesterday," Arianne says. "You lost it."

Even when he can't remember how he must have sinned against his daughter, she always makes him feel he deserves to be accused. "If you gave it to me," he says, "then it's somewhere in the house."

"I was supposed to turn it in today," Arianne says.

Bill is distracted by a light change. He has time to brake for the yellow light, but only if the driver behind him doesn't expect him to squeak through on the yellow. Reacting to a light change is no longer reflex but a futile attempt to read someone else's mind. He brakes, and the car rocks, and he can't help looking in the rearview mirror.

"Whoa, Dad!" Liam says. "You're scary."

Arianne's rump swooshes across the seat; her elbows go smackety-smack on vinyl. "My teacher says if I don't bring it in tomorrow, I can't go on the field trip."

"We'll find it," Bill says, trying to sound soothing. He has students like Arianne, kids who always rush into class late or are dismayed to discover that a paper is due or redden with humiliation when Bill gently corrects something they've said in class. These kids remind him of cartoon characters; every emotion registers on their faces as an abrupt infusion of shock, shame, or despair, and no mishap ever registers as less than catastrophe. It helps to divert them to task—have them scrawl the due date on a binder or open their books to the third chapter or answer the next question he's posed for discussion.

"We'll look for it as soon as we get home, and we'll put it in your backpack," Bill says.

"You don't remember what you did with it," Arianne says.

Bill's hands on the steering wheel seem to bear the weight of the wheel and the column that holds it in place. "Sure I do," Bill says.

Arianne kicks the back of the seat. The impact shudders up his spine.

As they approach the next intersection, the light turns yellow. The Jeep behind him is awfully close. But Bill brakes for the yellow light. In the rearview mirror he sees the Jeep grow rapidly larger till it blots out its own reflection. As the truck did when it hit him. Anticipation keens in Bill like hunger. The Jeep's tires squeal on the asphalt, and then the driver gives Bill the finger. When the light turns green, the driver of the Jeep leans on the horn.

Be reasonable, Bill tells himself.

Arianne wails. "You don't care about me! You don't care about anything! And now I won't get to go!"

Bill accelerates jerkily and careens into the left lane to get away from the Jeep, but the Jeep swerves with him. Bill slams the brake, though the light at the next intersection is still green. The Jeep's tires make a whining sound as it skids. Arianne emits a tiny squeak.

Bill doesn't mind that it hurts to twist around in his seat to look at Arianne. It should hurt. "Not another sound out of you," he says, "or you walk home."

She stares back at him in silence. But her body seems to vibrate and shimmer, to be blurred by the incessant needs that swarm about her. Bill has to remind himself, this is my daughter. My little girl.

He drives on, gripping the steering wheel, hunching over it in a way that he knows is not good for his back. When the Jeep swerves around him, he slows to let it pass. Be reasonable, be reasonable, he tells himself, until they arrive home. Pam pulls into the driveway right behind them, home early. She gets out of the car to wait for them, strands of fine hair drifting free of her ponytail, just like usual, her body quietly countering her strictness with it. Liam jumps from the car—the bang of the door, the slam of his backpack against it, so much announcement—to run to his mother. "Dad's a lousy driver," he hollers. Pam laughs and lifts him off his feet, and then she snags Arianne. She leans close so Arianne can snuggle against her and murmur and sniffle against her chest, and then she booms her answer, as loud as Liam's judgment of Bill's driving.

"No!" Pam says to Arianne. "She didn't say that, did she? That teacher is really an idiot! I'm going to have a talk with her."

Pam sends Arianne into the house to take her pick of the Godiva chocolates some realtor sent today (diverted to task, Bill thinks approvingly). How firmly in place Pam is, how simply her feelings are translated into deeds.

When Bill approaches her, Pam gives him a peck on the cheek.

"She whined the whole way home," Bill says. "She worries me." What he means is, she bothers me.

"You have to learn to ignore her. She's a twitchy kid, just like my brother was. She'll outgrow it someday." Pam laughs. "And she left her math book at school. She said you rushed her. I told her you'd go back for it."

Forty minutes, round-trip. Bill doesn't think he can do it. Anything could happen on the road at rush hour. He feels the way he felt behind the wheel of the car, as if things in his field of vision are arbitrarily swelling, bursting the constraints of perspective, and then shrinking back into place.

"With my back like this," he begins.

"I've got about eighty calls to make before I'm through for the day." Pam swats him lightly. "Just take a Vicodin when you get home."

Bill wakes in the night, his heart thudding. Why? He managed to retrieve the math book, Pam finished her calls in time to join them for dinner, and they watched TV afterward, relaxed. He lies still, soaking up the pain he feels whenever he wakes, the pain that seems to locate for him the parts of himself. He listens for some noise in the house, some clue to what woke him.

He decides to get up and check on things. He pulls on sweat-pants and a T-shirt and moves quietly through the house. He listens at the door of each kid's room. He looks in on Liam, curled in a ball at the foot of his bed, but when he tries Arianne's door, it opens only a few inches before he meets resistance. She has rigged up some kind of spiderweb of twine between the door and the doorjamb, with tape clumped here and there. He reaches in and feels for the doorknob, clotted with tape and twine. Don't ask, he tells himself. You don't want to know.

He goes to the front of the house and looks out the window at a silent street. He thinks about waking Pam. *Just take a Vicodin.* His back hurts enough that he'd have trouble going back to sleep anyway. Walking relieves his back pain. He could take a walk. He grabs Pam's clump of keys from the bowl by the door, and again something not exactly like intention directs him down the hill toward the empty house with these keys in his hand.

It's peaceful to be alone on the street with all these darkened houses around him. He could walk right up to anyone's windows and peer in. When he gets to the empty house, he has trouble locating the correct key on the key ring in the dark, and then he has a hard time fitting it into the lock.

He steps into the house and calls "hello?" into the echoing emptiness. And then he booms into the empty space, "Hello!" He flicks on the light switch in the living room. It's as naked as it was the first time he came. Pam hasn't gotten to work with her usual efficiency. His nostrils itch. Something about a house that's not lived in makes dust collect everywhere, silt the air. He has the urge to turn on every light as he moves through the house, to enter every room so that he can silt the air with himself. He flips one switch after another as he goes, on and off, opens closets and yanks on pull chains to light the naked bulbs inside, looks in the empty medicine cabinet in the bathroom, slides on the slick wooden floor of the hall as he heads toward the bedrooms. He finds a receipt wedged beneath a baseboard. He remembers packing up their old house. You always leave something behind, cannot completely erase the traces of your life within four walls.

He ends up in the kitchen, where all the cupboards are disappointingly empty. He turns on the tap and water pulses noisily from the faucet, forcing before it an explosive rush of air. When the water flows in a steady stream, he cups his hands to drink it. He lies down on the linoleum floor. The cold hard surface eases the ache in his back. He watches a branch scratch against the window above the sink. There's something drowsy-making about the fluid motion of the branch.

He wakes for the second time that night with a thudding heart. Only now he is blinded by light. That light seems so omnipotent and obliterating that the terse voice he hears seems to emanate from it, and he can't identify what is being said any more than he can identify any human source for it. A rough hand grips his shoulder and forces him over onto his stomach, yanking his hands behind his back.

The light no longer shines in his eyes. He can see the figure of a man—someone other than the man who has a knee on his back—in the kitchen doorway, the dark clothing, the peaked cap, the bulky outline of the belt that must hold a gun, another long-handled flashlight. He shouldn't have left lights on all over the house. He should say something to these men. Appease them.

He hears the clink of handcuffs being locked over his wrists. The sound of Pam's heavy watch ringing on her dresser, the sound of her clump of keys pinging when she drops them in the bowl. He wonders where he left the keys. He wonders what she'll do when his call wakes her. He blinks when the flashlight beam sweeps over him again, spiderwebbing his vision.

Why didn't he hear them trying the door, issuing an order into the silent house? And what intruder was his daughter expecting, preparing for, with the twine and tape Pam kept for packaging her gifts to the realtors?

The cop above him says something and tugs on Bill's shoulder. To comply, to get up from the floor, Bill has to fold his body to leverage his weight onto his knees. Pain balls up in Bill's lower back, a fist ready to strike, a separate existence within his existence.

Bill has that dizzy sensation he had when his back was x-rayed, a fearful and thrilling anticipation. He twists to get to his feet, deliberate now, anxious to force the torque in his spine, to flush from cover what's inside him.

thirteen ways
of looking
at a blackbird

I. When her son's life begins in her, Katie is stunned, not sure she can have this child, not with Malcolm, not when her life is still so tentative. Malcolm does not share her astonishment. He does what he always does before a gig, shares a joint in their living room with the guys in his band. Even stoned, Malcolm has a sharp-edged way of moving, a way of tumbling words as rapidly and effortlessly as he strikes keys on the piano. Katie hungers after that quality, feels pinched in comparison. When she does her work, it is work: whatever art is involved in her page layouts for the magazine must always be sacrificed to function.

When Malcolm lights another joint, the smell of the marijuana smoke makes her sick to her stomach. She makes out shapes in the haze, sees a predator stalking her, tendrils of smoke curved like claws. Until this moment she has thought of her wariness about drugs as a kind of cowardice, an inhibition. She has to leave the room. In the kitchen she kneels by the open window, gulping fresh air, engulfed by need narrowed to the contours of her own body.

II. Katie kisses Malcolm's beautiful shimmed-and-sheared hands, runs her tongue over the calluses on his fingers, playing them, their specific shapes and hardnesses, the way he plays piano. Pulling her against him on the sofa, Malcolm says he knew he would never have the technique for classical music. The kind of perfection required has to do with fitting yourself to the elegant, specific arrangement of the notes, not making mistakes. But jazz calls for exploring the gap between notes as written and what your fingers might accomplish in translating them into sound.

Trying to explain to her ignorant mind, her ignorant ears, he says, "Jazz comes from how you move in that space, back and forth. You don't disappear to make the music, you *are* the music. That's why you can take any piece of shit—like 'Someday My Prince Will Come'—and make it jazz. *If* you can."

Katie wants to be an artist because she wants to be good enough for Malcolm, something like him. Compared to her, he is an aristocrat. His parents were both college professors, and he grew up familiar with art history and classical music, took music lessons and trips to Europe as a matter of course. His carelessness about drugs is for her yet another example of privilege, another proof that he grew up in a world where there was room to take risk.

Katie thinks she hears the baby cry, and though Malcolm tries to hold onto her, she gets up to check. When she comes back with the baby, Malcolm is setting out the paraphernalia he needs to get high—the syringe, the spoon, the stub of a candle to heat the heroin to liquid state—with the elaborate care of the newly initiated. He's still flirting with the novelty of this, still free to be fascinated by how it's done.

She has tried not to worry about money or marrying now that they have the baby. Even their fights about drugs are careless blowups that seem to leave no residue except a faint afterglow of passion. She can't summon the energy to nag him again, anew, as if he's never promised to quit and never broken that promise before. In her arms her son is as heavy as the future, but she can still imagine that time's predictable rhythm can be thwarted by Malcolm's sheer inventiveness.

III. When Katie leaves Malcolm, it seems that every step she takes is a tiny one. She does layout for a newspaper four nights a week so that she can be with the baby for most of his waking hours. His days are orderly now, mealtimes and nap times scheduled by the clock. They spend mornings in the park, where Katie's vision contracts to the field of her child, the safety she must work to prove to him every day. She has mistaken so badly the margin for error.

When she starts seeing Billy, she tells him she does not want to get serious. She can carve out only a little time for Billy now that she is taking a class every week, working toward a teaching credential. But Billy brings Evan small presents that have to be dug from his pockets, wants to take them on picnics on Sunday afternoons, never arrives late and never leaves early. She feels for Billy nothing powerful enough to pull her to her knees, compel her against her will. When she thinks of being with him her thoughts run in a small circle. It's *nice* — he likes to hold hands; his bigness comforts her; he is honest in a way that thrills her, applying his conscience to everything from his work to the patient explanations he provides for her two-year-old's constant questions about why. He gives her similarly copious reasons when he asks her to marry him. There are two kinds of perfection.

IV. All through the night, Katie has been waking Evan, wiping his body with a damp washcloth, trying to bring the fever down. Evan, at six, has never had a high temperature before. She's often thought of his perfect health, like his perfect good temper, as something she earned through vigilance. When

Billy gets up and offers to trade places with her, give her a few hours of sleep, she refuses. Katie thought she'd feel less territorial after Maeve was born two years ago, but she doesn't. She still has that mother's superstition that she is irreplaceable.

Alone with Evan, she holds him in her arms in the battered rocking chair in his room, singing, listening to his whispery rasp, a metronome dictating the beating of her own heart, which ratchets with every catch in his breath. He's a heavy child, big-boned, much more like Billy than like his biological father. There's nothing in Evan of the wiriness, the abrupt, jerky energy of Malcolm.

Evan's eyes flutter open, and he sighs *mommy* as if she's a place he's momentarily waking to recognize. He murmurs something else, tenderly. *Popsicle.* He doesn't want one actually but is just, deliriously, anticipating pleasure. The children's sick days are sweet rituals — they get Popsicles, they get to watch the TV that is otherwise kept in the closet like a shameful secret, they get to drink weak tea from tiny teacups, laden with milk and sugar, they are allowed to nap on the sofa surrounded by toys. All the routines of their household are adapted to the small orbit of a child's delights, from the fussy way they make toast and jam into treats that Evan calls "riders" to their gleeful bedtime dances with stuffed animals. Every day amazes Katie, such richness in place of the hard life, the work and struggle and penance, she expected.

The raging heat of Evan's body burns her own skin as she holds him. She's afraid he'll have convulsions. She's afraid she has hesitated too long already, that she and Billy should have taken him to the hospital hours ago. The same animal instinct that gives her such certainty when it comes to what her children need — that stretches like a taut cord between her and them, a physical tug she can feel in her spine, her ribs — betrays her, pulls her into humiliating helplessness.

By the time she wakes Billy, she's sobbing that he has to get dressed and drive them to the hospital. In her arms, Evan stirs from lethargy to cry with her. Billy gets out of bed and takes Evan from her. "Sh," he says, "you're scaring him." He carries Evan to the bathroom to turn on the shower. "It's only croup," he tells her. He holds Evan carefully, comfortably, as the steam from the hot shower clouds the bathroom, and when their child begins to breathe more easily, Billy carries him back to bed and tucks him in. "I'll stay with him for a while," Billy says. He's sending her away because there's something dangerous in her. She sees that Billy doesn't love as she does, that it isn't necessary for love to be shadowed by treacherous dread.

V. In one way Malcolm has disappeared from her life; in another way, he is always there. Over the years she's heard about him from people who were once his friends. "He went down," one of them told her. Everyone wanted to banish him for having slipped from improvisational daring into the imprisoning need of the addict. No one ever seemed to know how it had happened.

Once in a while Malcolm calls her. She can't imagine how he finds her phone number, as indifferent as he is to the world beyond the compacted core of his need. But he calls. She has learned not to panic when she picks up the phone and hears him say her name, learned that she doesn't really exist for him, not in a way that he can sustain past the impulse to dial her number. *How you doing, how's my son, that's good, real good, see you around.*

Malcolm is gone. Gone in the same way that the youthful mistakes of her friends are gone—the love affairs that retrospective has turned into comedy or a bitter lesson, the foolish and romantic political commitments, the experiments with sex or cocaine somehow equivalent now that they can be looked on with a degree of wry amusement, coated over with irony. The past is gone, even for Billy, who had his heady days as a young socialist but only gently revised this former self. He went to law school, but he works for a union, the same union where his father was once a steward, and he puts in long hours for little money. He is not ironic about Katie's big mistake, but he is gentle and lenient in a way that excuses her and makes her feel ashamed of the impulse to reclaim Malcolm from the shabby and venial seediness Billy assumes.

Malcolm is not gone. Even though he's seen Evan only once since Katie left him. When they received the final papers for Billy to adopt Evan, Malcolm refused to sign unless Katie brought Evan to see him. She was eight months pregnant with Maeve, and she and Billy had just bought a house, and she felt that Malcolm had called her to him to dispense one final curse that could pull her life down around her like a house of cards.

Four-year-old Evan was afraid even of Malcolm's apartment building, the halls that stank of urine and canned beans heated on a hot plate and a nameless sourness. Malcolm answered his door and ushered them in with such liquid grace that Katie knew he was high, and Evan refused to go to him when Malcolm sat on the edge of the bed and beckoned him with his long musician's fingers.

For a moment, Katie expected those fingers to conjure music out of thin air. When they lived together, Katie and Malcolm squeezed a grand piano into their small apartment, and sometimes while Malcolm played, Katie would lie beneath the piano, in the belly of the music, where the vibration of the wires was stronger than the notes themselves, their hum a wave of jarred molecules that she could feel striking her skin.

Malcolm had a present for Evan, an old-fashioned mechanical toy of stamped metal, a brightly colored bird whose stiff forked legs stamped on Malcolm's palm when he wound it up. When he leaned forward to hand the bird to Evan, Evan shrank back against Katie and began to cry. "I don't want it to bite me," he said.

Katie will see, forever, that bird, so intricately painted, cupped in the palm of Malcolm's hand, the gift he offered: the grace of her life measured intently against his ruin. She took the bird when Evan would not.

VI. Maeve comes to Katie in tears, so overwhelmed by her anger that she can't talk. Finally Maeve finds words for her heartbreak. Evan said she wasn't his real sister.

Katie cuddles Maeve, reassures her that her brother didn't mean to insult her. Mommy and Daddy have explained this before, remember? It's just a technicality—which is a *what?* Maeve wants to know—and it only means that Evan had a different father than Maeve, though Billy is their real father now. Then Katie calls Evan into the bedroom so she can ask him in private to account for himself.

Evan shrugs. "It's true. She's only my half sister. She doesn't even look like me."

"Does that bother you sometimes?"

He gives her an eleven-year-old's best attempt at a withering look. "It's just a fact."

His dogged rationality about everything can be so paper-thin—the government should force people to conserve energy by taxing them for driving cars; it makes no sense for his mother to fuss about how messy his room is when it's neater than the rooms of any of his friends; his father is a neutral bit of biological data.

Billy stops in the doorway. "What's going on?" he says. "Maeve's all bent out of shape. You didn't hit her, did you, Evan?"

"Evan said she was only his half sister," Katie says. "He hurt her feelings."

"Maybe it was the way you said it," Billy says. "Your sister worships you. You might consider lowering the daily quota of insults, intended or not."

Billy doesn't imagine there's more to this than the usual bickering, and for a moment Katie is embarrassed by her impulse to ferret out some unspoken worry, to badger Evan in pursuit of her craving to speak of Malcolm, to tell herself that story with tenderness and regret. But being Evan's mother has schooled her in self-restraint.

She turns to Evan. "You know you can always ask us about your father."

"It's not like he's really my father or anything," Evan says. "I don't even know him. And I'm almost grown-up now. It's too late."

Evan is safe, immune to her longing. The pain of his beginning has taken on the proportions of beauty recollected, faded to a sweet ghostly undertone.

VII. At the end of the art period, as they finish their chalk drawings, the third-graders bring them to Katie, touching her with their dusty fingers to get her attention, clamoring for praise, which is easy for her to give. She loves kids' artwork. For them, no mental construct intrudes between emotion and thing; their drawings always betray the beautiful, unique distortions of what they really see. It's what Katie lacks and why she was right to become a teacher instead of struggling to mere competence as a graphic designer. Her love for her own children, indistinguishable from her pride in their flourishing selves, made her think, this is my gift, why not use it? She finds it as hard to distinguish between pride in her students and pride in herself for their class projects—lanterns made from elaborately cut milk cartons and tissue paper, Balinese-style puppets of paper and wood, carved dried gourds strung with beads to make musical instruments.

She takes a drawing from someone's hand, and when she looks over the edge of the paper, she is surprised to discover the owner is Maeve. A possessive swell of joy takes her by surprise—as it does a dozen times a day—but she cannot scoop Maeve into her arms at school. She and Billy debated whether it was good for the kids to be assigned to the alternative public school where she teaches, but it's a good school, a real community, and the kids suffer only from a sweet shyness when they come to her art class.

Maeve's vivid drawing of a horse plucks Katie from her perch of professional admiration. Maeve loves horses, begged them to pay for riding lessons. Billy and Katie vie to take her to the stable just to exist within the aura of Maeve's delight, which is Maeve's gift, so easily expressed in the fluid parabolic lines of her drawing.

Katie murmurs, "It's beautiful," holds herself to this quick intimation of her feelings. She might hurt Maeve if she dared to betray her genuine awe, might burden her with extravagant expectations. But Maeve looks at her as if she is waiting for more.

Katie has the same habits for keeping order at home as she does at school. She and Billy pay conscientious attention to everything from bedtime and snacks to teaching the children about recycling and table manners. She used to be someone more careless, expansive, when she was with Malcolm, but that other self, a stranger, seems like an accident, temporarily and mysteriously shaped by circumstances. Maybe the bulky solidity of her life now, the quantity of care it takes to ward off chance, shapes her just as arbitrarily, and she is no more a virtuous wife and mother than she was an adventurer. Maybe she only imagines that Maeve hangs on her arm for an extra moment, waiting for more from her when she can't afford to drift across the borders of the straight and narrow.

VIII. Evan starts to have headaches when he turns twelve. He doesn't complain. Only when the headache is so fierce that he can't eat or has to lie down in the dark will he ask for Tylenol.

Evan's pediatrician refers them to a neurologist. The neurological workup shows no obvious physical cause. The neurologist asks if there's a history of migraines in the family, because the onset sometimes occurs at adolescence, and Katie can supply only half of Evan's medical history. The doctor questions Evan about whether he is happy at school and whether he feels pressure to get good grades.

Katie takes Evan to another doctor. For a few months, their lives are a round of tests—allergy skin tests, more neurological scans, blood work—and experiments with different medications—ergotamine, sumatriptan, Fiorinal.

Nothing works, and Evan doesn't complain, which shames Katie. Once when he was seven, he punched Katie's arm, and he only looked at her when she lectured him about hitting. Goaded by his indifference, she kept after him all day, claiming he'd bruised her. That night, he got out of bed and came to find her, sobbing that he hadn't meant to hurt her. And she felt terrible for not having recognized the remorse in his silence, his sealed shame. She doesn't want to fail him again.

She takes him to another neurologist for another round of tests. When they arrive for their follow-up appointment, this doctor talks about how migraines are caused by a kind of misfiring in the brain and prescribes a tiny dose of a tricyclic antidepressant that sometimes corrects this chemical deficiency.

Katie says, "That's enough," and yanks Evan up out of the chair. She shakes on the drive home, with Evan beside her saying, "Mom, calm down."

When they get home, she finds Billy in the kitchen starting dinner. She asks him to come to the bedroom so they can talk, and then after she carefully shuts the door, she lets her fury spill over.

"That asshole prescribed antidepressants," she says. "He just wants to put Evan on more horrible drugs instead of figuring out what's wrong. I want him to order a CAT scan, but he won't."

"Maybe that's not the point anymore," Billy says. "Maybe there isn't a specific reason, and the best thing we can do is just help Evan learn to live with it."

"Live with it? You sound just like that doctor. Who cares why he has to suffer?"

"He has mild headaches," Billy says. "He's not *suffering*."

"Yes, he is!" She and Evan are alone in this.

Billy mistakes her tears of anger for tears of weakness. He takes her in his arms, speaks soothingly. "You've dragged him to enough doctors. Now you start talking about CAT scans. You're not doing him any good. You've got to get hold of yourself."

Held in his arms, she is compressed to a shape dictated by his muscles, his bones, his reach.

She wants to hit him. "We haven't tried everything. There's acupuncture. There's biofeedback."

"Biofeedback isn't a bad idea," Billy says. Even his gentleness can't disguise his lawyer's instinct to seek compromise, negotiate a settlement instead of a trial date. Her panic bangs against the sturdy slope of his body like a bird against a window, smacking itself inert. The grief she wants to feel for this small corpse may even be what makes her press her mouth so fiercely to his.

IX. When the phone rings, Maeve jumps up to get it, nearly knocking over the chessboard. She loves to answer the phone. When she speaks into the mouthpiece, she enunciates her lines like an actress, oozes etiquette and politeness. "May I ask who is calling please?"

She puts a hand over the mouthpiece, then bellows in her real voice, "Mom, it's some man for you."

When Katie takes the phone from Maeve, Malcolm speaks a quiet hello into her ear. "Who answered the phone?" he says.

"That was my daughter."

"I thought—at first, you know—that it might be him."

"Evan's voice is changing," Katie says. "It's much deeper than Maeve's."

"Maeve. That's a pretty name."

"Just a second." Katie untangles the phone cord and backs into the kitchen from the dining room. She looks at her family before she closes the door on the cozy vision at the table: Billy and Evan leaning over the chessboard, their elbows on the table, Evan warning Maeve that if she doesn't move her bishop, it will be threatened by her dad's knight, and Maeve, tiny distillation of fierceness, hotly answering that she knows that, he doesn't have to tell her everything.

"How are you, Malcolm?" Katie says.

"Good," he says. "I'm good. I'm in rehab now. I've been in rehab for two years."

She wants him to tell her what he wants. Instead, she says, "That's good news."

"Well, you know, you take it one day at a time."

"Uh-huh."

"I was wondering if I could see you sometime," he says. "Just to talk."

Katie is glad that Billy and the children can't see her cowering over the mouthpiece of the phone. Up until now, she has been conning herself, the way she and Billy are always conning the children, translating all the sticky and unpleasant truths of the world into patient, tolerant restatements of the facts: warnings about strangers whittled down to mild guidelines about who to talk to when and the reassurance that most people are nice, the ugly facts of prejudice translated into a mingled contempt and pity for people governed by ignorance and fear. Malcolm is a pair of headlights bearing down on Katie in the dark.

X. When Katie peers in through the window of the cafe, she recognizes Malcolm right away. Reflexively she compares him with Billy: Malcolm, still wiry, sits on the chair as if he must concentrate in order to keep still instead of flying up from where he's perched; Billy can place his body anywhere, standing or sitting, and seem instantly, organically rooted to the spot, moving with smoothness from the fulcrum of an essential calm.

When she approaches the table, Malcolm jerks up, half rising from his chair and then falling back as if it's a grievous error to be startled so easily. She might not have recognized him if she had only his face to go by—its lines and creases have been sharpened by the taut, collapsed skin; his teeth are a dull, yellowish brown; his eyes bobble with the mechanical instability of a doll's.

He surprises her by reaching out to shake her hand. His hands are cool and dry to the touch and too big for his body. Oh, she remembers him always having to arrange those big hands, find somewhere to put them, as if they were extra possessions.

He says he appreciates her willingness to see him. It's been so long; it's not like he isn't fully aware of what he did to her and their son.

"And you're looking so good, you sure don't need me around," he says. His words flicker and dart like his eyes, a zigzag of tangled false starts and sudden shifts of direction. "But the thing is—when you're stable, when you're ready, um, you got to make amends, and I've been straight for two years, I don't need to tell you what a job that's been, and I wonder about him, you know, my blood, my son, somewhere in the world, and I don't even know the first thing, which I have no right to ask, I forfeited that right, I know that."

Katie feels as if she's clutching her middle-class self in her lap like a big, bulging purse. Malcolm's jerky mannerisms aren't even organized enough to be termed nervousness, and he is afraid of her, afraid of all the armor that living in the world, thriving in it, has granted her. She plans to tell Billy about this visit after the fact, when it's taken care of. He'd have offered too many good reasons why she should have refused Malcolm, and she could not have accounted for her *yes*.

"Evan's fine," Katie says. "He's a great kid. Levelheaded, smart, sweet."

"And how are things going for you?" Malcolm says.

"Things are good," Katie says. "I'm an art teacher. I work with little kids."

"I remember that," Malcolm says vaguely. "You wanted to be an artist."

"What about you?" Katie says. "Do you still play?"

He watches his hands fumble with his coffee cup, shred the napkin beside it. "No. That's gone."

He presses his palms flat to the table in order to keep them still. "I'm a counselor at a clinic. I go to schools, give talks, lead groups for people in recovery."

"I'm glad you're OK," Katie says.

"Man, I got to go through an incredible amount of orthodontic work. Horse rots your teeth." He laughs. "But one good thing, out of all this—surprise, surprise—I was always careful about needles, never shared. A good middle-class kid after all."

She's forgotten, till now, Malcolm's bitter amusement at anything conventional, at her small efforts at domesticity when they shared an apartment. A once familiar expression bobs on the surface of his eroded face and then disappears.

"I did wonder why you wanted to see me," she says.

His eyes flicker to avoid hers. "The people you've hurt—you're supposed to make amends. I know I've got to prove I'm on the level and all that."

She sees that he has no idea how to ask her for anything or what to ask her for. She has spent the last ten years ready to protest to him, "Yes, this life is good." But he hasn't been the one arguing with her. He has no claim to lay on her.

XI. When Katie and Maeve get home from Maeve's riding lesson, Maeve insists on boasting to Billy and Evan about how she was thrown. Maeve was cantering around the perimeter of the riding ring, the instructor standing at the center calling out instructions, when Maeve's horse began to buck. He threw her over his head and then jumped her prone body, loose reins flying.

Evan says, "Mom must have had a heart attack."

"I'm proud of her," Maeve says. "She behaved herself."

When she saw Maeve thrown, Katie didn't cry out. She didn't run into the ring. She watched the instructor catch the horse, lead him to Maeve, question Maeve about whether she was hurt. When Maeve got to her feet and smiled at Katie, Katie made herself smile back.

Billy looks at Katie and laughs. "Honey, it's OK. She's all in one piece."

Evan comes to give Katie a hug. At thirteen, he has suddenly grown bigger than Katie, and it is so amazing to be held by him, to feel the thick cord of muscles in his arms, the man-sized bones of his shoulders. "Poor Chicken Little," he says.

Yes, Katie felt terrified. But she can't admit what else she felt—the adrenaline rush when it was over, when the instructor helped Maeve back on the horse. The threat, sudden and literal, immediately evoked its countermeasure of joy, an exultant traitor to Katie's every maternal instinct.

Billy winks at Maeve. "Your mom's not going to make it through your next lesson."

"Why don't you all get off my back?" Katie says.

She thinks, no one here knows me. Her real self moves shiftily behind the screen of *mommy-honey*. She's snuck off to see Malcolm. She's clung to him as talisman, proof that she can slip free of this life: delicious fear, thrilling vice of the wicked, and no timid little weakness.

XII. Evan lies on the couch with another headache, and Katie tries to talk him through an amateurish, patched-together version of hypnosis, about the only benefit they've gained from all the trips to all the different kinds of doctors.

She asks Evan to breathe slowly and deeply, imagine that rhythm as the rhythm of his pulse.

He opens one eye. "That's just not—it's not anatomically correct."

"Sh," she says. He always begins these sessions with a token avowal of his skepticism. He takes his cue from Billy, who implies in a hundred ways that these sessions are Katie's way of making herself feel better. Evan couldn't learn biofeedback because he couldn't learn to recognize subtle signals from his body, couldn't pay the right kind of attention. It will take her ten minutes of quiet talk to get him to relax the tense muscles of his body, relinquish control.

She tells him to imagine the beat of his pulse sending blood lapping out from his heart, one wave after another in steady rhythm. If a thought comes to him, it's only tossed by those waves. She describes the tide slowly rising, flowing to the tips of his fingers, his toes, its warmth molding his body as if it were soft wax.

When she has tried this on Maeve, Maeve actually gets sleepy. Evan will usually deny it's had much effect, though often by the end of a session the migraine tightness has left the skin around his eyes.

She finishes the way she always does. "You have to remember what this feels like after you open your eyes. The steadiness at the core of you. When you start to feel a headache coming on, this is where you have to come. Just listen to the waves."

She watches Evan breathe evenly and deeply. Maybe the curl of his fingers is a degree or two less tight. Once when he was about seven, she and Billy sat down with him to try to explain about his father. They'd rehearsed exactly how to present the story, how to lie. After their nonjudgmental declaration of facts, Evan said, "So my other dad—he was like the bad guy, right?" They had to explain everything all over again. As if that raw feeling could be amended instead of chased into hiding. But honesty runs counter to love. Katie doesn't want her son to learn he has lost a father. She doesn't believe in any steadiness at the core.

XIII. Katie agrees to see Malcolm again, and again she does not tell Billy. They meet in the same restaurant, both of them so taken up with the task of seeing one another that they can't spare the energy to care much about the details. She means to tie things up neatly this time if she can.

They try to make small talk and fail. Malcolm can't think of any questions to ask her beyond simple ones. His knee keeps knocking the table; he keeps clenching his fingers around his coffee cup, making the spoon tremble against the saucer.

He works his jaw back and forth as if he is rolling a marble around in his mouth. "Does he ever ask about me?"

She wishes Malcolm would refer to Evan by name. "No."

"Of course the kid doesn't have any use for me—I guess, you know, I'm still a long way from thinking straight. I live in a studio, I go down to the clinic every day, just how I used to when I was a client, junkies, ex-junkies, it's the same old, same old, and I'm just trying to think of how to do this at all, how you pick up your life again, what that is, you know, like what do people do on Saturdays, and how do you ask a woman out, and what is it you're supposed to do when it's your mother's birthday."

She's ashamed of her own scruples, her mistrust of the plentiful confusion of memory, so clouded by wishes, when Malcolm is forced to improvise from scratch.

He's drained his cup nearly to the bottom. He starts tearing open sugar packets and slowly pouring them into the cup. One, two, three, four packets slowly silt into the cup, and then he stirs the sugar and coffee into a grainy sludge.

She would like to offer him something to take hold of. "You used to steal sugar packets from restaurants," she says.

"Did I?" he says.

"You'd leave them in your pockets, and I'd throw your pants in the wash, and when it was done, there'd be streaks of sugar paste on the clothes, tiny bits of paper sticking to everything."

She watches his face for some sign of interest in himself, some willingness to believe with her that she loved him crazily. "We had glorious fights, remember?"

He smiles at her with such humility. "I wasn't so good with the baby, was I?"

She feels trapped by knowing too little and too much to make sense of anything. She remembers sleeping beside Malcolm, who'd fallen into bed fully clothed, stupefied, and then waking in the darkness to the sound of the baby crying, Malcolm no longer beside her. The baby's crying stopped, abruptly smothered. She jumped from bed, raced to find them. In the kitchen Malcolm was standing by the sink, the baby in his arms. He'd turned on the tap, and the baby was holding perfectly still, eyes wide, mesmerized into silence by the tinkling of the running water. She would never have thought to try that.

Malcolm says, "I'm always seeing the kids in the park, fooling with their skateboards, and I wonder if he's one of them, and I don't even know it."

What yearning there might be in his words is faint, pitifully impoverished.

"He doesn't skateboard," she says.

"Do you think he would see me?"

She can't bear to refuse him outright. "I don't know."

She reaches under the table for her purse. She always keeps pictures in there, loose, and she plucks them out for him.

Malcolm looks at a picture of Katie holding both the kids in her arms, all of them laughing, no one looking at the camera, and then studies a more recent photo of Billy with an arm thrown over Evan's shoulder.

"He's that big?" Malcolm says in surprise.

"Evan takes after my father's side of the family," Katie says.

With every word she does a poorer job of describing Evan to Malcolm. She thinks at first it's because the pictures are so very middle-class—taken at beach resorts, their cozy home, parks, school festivals. Then she's scared that she might be inventing Evan as uncertainly as she has reimagined Malcolm, her own past. In her mouth her son thins—a baseball fan, always in sweatpants, never ready for school on time—till he could be any of those boys with skateboards. She lacks some gift. She feels she is taking a guess at her son the way Malcolm must guess what he can't remember about the habits of daily life. How can a habit as persistent as love leave no clear notation, no record of itself other than this wavering approximation?

"I sure would like to know my son," Malcolm says.

Poor Malcolm can't imagine what a daunting proposition that is. When will there be some right time for Evan to feel the hurt his father has caused him, to face this ruined man, to reconstitute himself according to loss? What words, what story could prepare him or make him understand the life Katie was willing to wish on him when he was born? She is visited by the same sudden and absurd relief she felt after Maeve was thrown by the horse. If only for a moment, she feels not braced against herself. She pulls out her wallet to show Malcolm the only other photo she has, of Evan at four, standing before an easel, his hands dipped to the wrists in red paint.

What's ahead will be hard in ways Katie has trained herself to anticipate, but maybe there'll be gaps like this one when it's also something else, when she can hear another music murmuring.

roam the wilderness

"O brother, dear brother, why are

they absolving me instead

of my brother?"

The Epic of Gilgamesh, Tablet VII

In the letter he wrote to each of them, he mentioned his brother's death. He worked hard on the sentences that described his feelings, constructed them, even though the feelings were true. Sam's car accident had cleaved Marshall's life as abruptly as it had cleaved his brother's; afterward he felt old, too old for the life he was leading. He applied to graduate school and gave notice to the park service, and now he has a few months free before he starts at the University of California in Santa Cruz. He has planned his trip according to who did and did not reply to his letters, his route a track retracing the old byways of his heart, circumventing lacunae where contact had been broken or former heat had dissipated to nothing.

Some of these women he hasn't seen since college, others were buddies in the park service, temporarily stationed out on the Olympic Peninsula with him, and some were briefly lovers. The line between lover and friend has always confused him; he has a string of women friends whose feelings for him have long been tinged with the erratic bitterness of unrequited love and another string of former lovers whom he has ardently pummeled into remaining friends. He has written to a few male friends too, but his route is dictated by women, with whom intimacy has always been so easy.

Isabelle in Ashland is his first stop. He drives into the theater district, where the summer Shakespeare festival's buildings have been set down like giant blocks in what would otherwise be a peaceful, rural Oregon town. He wanders among the tourists and stops at an ice cream parlor to get directions to the tree-shaded street where Isabelle lives. When he arrives at her little house, she isn't back from rehearsals yet, and he waits for her on the front porch, finishing his ice cream. He looks in the window at a worn sofa with a pine chest before it, old standing lamps with fringed shades, candles clustered on the windowsill, their melted wax frozen in the flow of a spill. He is glad she's not home yet, so he can indulge in anticipation, in imagining this life he is about to waltz into on his way to somewhere else.

When Isabelle arrives, she jumps from her beat-up bike and rushes at him, her long, straight black hair floating behind her. She throws herself into his arms and kisses him on the mouth, and he remembers that what most drew him to her was her theatricality, the glorious excess of emotion that always left him wondering what was and wasn't real in her. He smells some botanical concoction in her hair, imbibes the warmth of her through the shiny fabric of her multicolored shirt, and when she leans back from him, bracing herself with her arms around his waist, he can feel an erection stirring.

His brother's death has lifted him into an intensity of emotion that brings unearned gifts: each moment seems crystalline, slowed so that he can take in everything, from the sweet fog of scents rising from Isabelle's skin to the snub-nosed pressure of her hipbone against his. Even when he feels blindsided by grief, the world seems newly lit.

Isabelle punches his arm. "It's been four years, and you don't look a day older."

Inside the house he admires the African masks hung on the wall. Isabelle waves her hand dismissively. "They're not mine," she says, disappointing him. "This place gets passed around among the people who come out for the summer theater. Sort of slowly silts up with a little bit of everyone who's passed through."

They cook dinner together, grilling a thick salmon steak, washing dirt off lettuce from the garden that is haphazardly maintained by the successive tenants of the house. Isabelle, with her heavy eye makeup and shiny shirt, seems out of place in the homely kitchen, searching the drawers for a good knife as if she doesn't live here. She complains about having to scrounge for work when she goes home to New York City. But she prefers the democratic struggle of the stage to commercial work.

"That's what's great about these summer companies," she says, her hands flaring as she talks. "I've only got a small part in *The Winter's Tale*, but in rehearsals all of us argue about lines, interpretation — it's invigorating."

Marshall asks for an example, hungry for real information. And soon Isabelle is arguing her opinion to him. The basic secret of the play is that it's a tearjerker, that at the end, when what the king believes to be a statue of his dead wife turns out to be the living woman, capable of forgiving him, the actors ought to be able to look past the lights and see tears shining on the faces of the people in the audience.

"That's what theater is essentially about," Isabelle says. "Giving that audience a free ride on the emotion you're digging up."

When they finish the second bottle of red wine, Isabelle yawns and says she's tired. She offers to fold out the sofa bed for Marshall, but he says it isn't necessary. "I don't sleep well these days."

Isabelle takes his hand. "I didn't want to bring it up," she says. "You know. You feel you're causing pain if you say anything."

"It's hard for me to talk about Sam," Marshall says. "I think about him a lot."

He lies awake at night, not remembering his brother but rehearsing him, replaying a gesture in his mind to get it right, growing less and less sure with each effort. The joke's on him, the philosophy major who gleefully used the tools of his training in logic to demonstrate that no one could prove anything. He no longer has time for the self-defeating history of philosophy, the laborious parsing of the world into fewer and fewer certainties. Now when morning finds him still lying awake, he studies how dawn's light etches the fan of tendons on the back of his outstretched hand, and he marvels at his power to command his fingers to wriggle. He's eager to begin his graduate work in biology, where every fact or nuance uncovered connects to another, snaps into place in an intricate gridwork of profusion.

Instead of going to bed, Isabelle opens another bottle of red wine. She describes the tiny apartment she shares in Manhattan with her boyfriend Ross, the tub that sits in the kitchen. Marshall deflects Isabelle's curiosity about his job in the park service. When he left college, he'd felt noble for not marching off to law school or med school or business school like so many of his classmates. He wanted to head to the woods like Thoreau. But he doesn't like to talk about those six years he spent in the park service, giving people directions when they couldn't read the trail maps, preparing little talks on wildlife that he delivered in a corny outdoor theater, living in the housing complex that was just like a college dorm, participating in pranks with his coworkers, who left the park only to make the trek into Seattle for a weekend. He's willing to talk about now, his hope that he can become a field biologist. He still believes in the woods.

Sometime in the early hours of the morning, Isabelle puts down her wine glass and lies on the sofa and puts her head in his lap. He strokes her hair. She asks him why they never got together when they met years ago.

Marshall had been in love with another ranger. He saw Isabelle only on weekends in Seattle, where she roomed with a mutual friend. "I was with someone then."

Isabelle laughs. "You weren't married."

Marshall came close only once. His college girlfriend, Kay, had wanted Marshall to marry her. Even then Marshall had taken very seriously his obligation to be monogamous—had bypassed so many opportunities—but when they graduated and the future so suddenly became the present, he hadn't known how to say yes or no to Kay. She'd gone home to St. Louis to look for a job, and he'd gone out West. They'd written each other love letters, pretended for a year that they were still in a relationship. They never actually decided to break up, just mysteriously crossed the threshold into affection and nostalgia. He was a groomsman at her wedding.

"Well, I really lusted after you," Isabelle says. "I've always wondered what it would have been like." She touches his cheek. "Wouldn't you like to find out?"

"Your boyfriend," Marshall says.

"We're theater people," she says. "We're loose. As long as you use a condom."

Their sex is simple, clean, almost like exercise. The bed creaks and groans beneath them for what seems like hours, and their bodies turn slippery with sweat, and they keep at it and keep at it. Marshall thinks that if they'd made love so long ago, the act would have been encumbered by his guilt and Isabelle's indulgence in emotion, would have been only a first step toward trouble. Now it's an uncomplicated mixture of curiosity and hard work. Her breasts are as firm as he had imagined they would be, small, stippled by goose bumps, and he wants to mouth, again and again, the sweet swoop from her hip bones to the swell of her abdomen, take into himself the answer to his curiosity.

Minus any complicating wants, he feels free to focus entirely on admiring her, as if for the first time, finding in her features, the too-large eyes and mobile mouth, something surpassing the anonymous beauty that would have steered her career in the direction of TV and movies. And she returns his admiration as easily. "Jesus Christ, but you're beautiful," she says. In the mystery of her nakedness he discovers fragments of the past, the innocent way that he and Isabelle used to hold hands. After he slowly and carefully eases out of her body, she kisses his ear and whispers that she knew he'd be like a kid. He lies on his stomach beside her, an arm thrown over her breasts, and falls asleep.

He doesn't wake till noon, long after Isabelle has risen, made coffee, read the paper. Together they make a huge breakfast, and Isabelle piles it all onto one plate and sits in his lap, feeding him toast from her hand, trading bites of scrambled eggs from a single fork. He teases her into going rafting on the Rogue River. Only a degenerate New Yorker could live here and not partake of the wilderness.

But it's a mistake. The cold water sloshing in the bottom of the raft numbs Isabelle's feet, and she's afraid she'll fall out every time they make a run through white water. Marshall can't understand. The need to work each time they hit white water doesn't leave any room to be afraid. Like the work of rock climbing. His brother taught him. When they were rappelling each other up the sheer face of a granite cliff, they could think only of the smallest things, the clink of a hook being clipped to the line, the rocketing scatter of pebbles beneath a misplaced foot, the blisters the braided line rubbed onto their palms. The smallest mistake that either of them made could cost the other his life, the two lives made one by the line that linked them. When they reached the top, their skin was infused with the rosy afterglow of the climb.

He feels that same exhilaration on the river. But when they finally pull out of the water, Isabelle can't hide the fact that she's had to make herself endure the last four hours. She huddles on the drive home, shivering, but he makes it up to her. He draws a bath for her, peels off her wet clothes that stink of river water, brings her a hot cocoa in the tub, and then massages her legs and numb feet. When she complains that he smells like the river too, he shucks his own clothes and squats in the tub to wash her hair, kneads her scalp till the lather turns creamy, till he can trace rivulets of foam down the taut tendons at the back of her neck and over her sharp narrow shoulders. She turns her face away when he leans to kiss her, but he persists, pulls her into a slick embrace.

They have another two days of perfection, big meals, many bottles of wine, hearty activity in bed that leaves them both aching, walking stiffly. He feels so pleased now by how concrete, how real, the physical consequences of pleasure are. The night before he has to go, when Isabelle is lying in his arms and he can feel sleep tugging at him, he asks her if she'll come with him down the coast. He wants to drive through the redwoods of Northern California on his way down to Santa Cruz.

"I don't like to camp," Isabelle says.

"That's because you've never tried it."

"You know I can't," she says.

He's afraid for a moment that he's ruined everything, marred the wholeness of these days. But then she kisses him tenderly, and this emotion, sweeter than regret, seals their victory over the incompleteness of the past.

All the next day, as he drives west to the coast, he can smell the stench of river mud in the car—from her wet clothes, from her skin and hair. She's with him, as his brother is with him, his ashes sealed in a tin canister tucked under the seat.

He arrives at Lisa's at dusk. She's still in uniform, a ranger at the Oregon Caves. Lisa lives with her lover, Susan, but when he worked with Lisa at the Olympic National Park, she was often lonely like him. The park staff was such a small and transitory social group that anyone who was single could go months between relationships, and Lisa had the added complication that she was gay—she used to joke that a lesbian who didn't live in a city deserved to be sex deprived. They cemented their friendship by sharing pranks like dirty little secrets—they coated the hall floors of their apartment building with Vaseline in the middle of the night and denied responsibility, sewed sergeant's stripes on the sleeves of their tight-assed boss's uniform. Marshall sometimes slept over with Lisa, who wore a bulky flannel gown that prohibited exploration but enriched their mutual curiosity, made tantalizing the fact that they would never have sex with each other.

He wants Lisa to haul him into her bed again, but Susan regards him with mistrust the moment he steps in the door. She sits with her hand in Lisa's lap while they drink beer, watching them both, eyes narrowed. When Susan gets up to go to bed, she stands in the doorway waiting until Lisa joins her, eyes downcast, and he has to unroll his sleeping bag on their sofa and lie awake all night.

The next day he takes Lisa's tour of the caves, but she is schoolmarmish and strict about not touching the moist, cool walls of the cave, addresses everyone, including him, as sir or ma'am. At the end of her tour, she refuses to play hooky and explore the woods with him. He goes back to her house, chops a cord of wood for her and Susan, and stacks it neatly on the porch of their cabin. He sweats out the fantasy that he can win Susan over, that when the two women come home, he'll be welcome to share a bed with both of them. At dusk they return, carrying dinner in a paper sack and a video. At their kitchen table, littered with greasy paper and beer bottles, Susan talks about work the way that he and Lisa used to talk about work, for insiders only. Then Susan puts the video on, and they watch it in silence. In the morning, after the women leave for work, he bakes chocolate chip cookies and leaves a plate of them on the table with a good-bye note.

A few hours after Marshall drives over the state line into California, he sees billboards along the highway: See the Ancient Giants! Redwoods! He feels awe for redwoods, vaulting into the sky the way they vault through time, spanning centuries recorded only as narrow rings in their mighty circumference. He pulls over where the signs direct him and parks. It's a private preserve, with a ticket booth where he hastily hands over money, his mind on getting into the woods, roaming the wilderness. But immediately he realizes he's been conned. A paved path winds past trees that are necklaced by signs bearing cartoon-like animals painted on plywood. Approaching a tree, he comes within hearing range of the tape-recorded message that plays from a small metal box staked into the ground beside the path. A saccharine voice exudes enthusiasm about the tree and tells him the name it's been given. The tiny grove buzzes with the gnat-like sound of these recordings.

He imagines the path will continue past this odious Disneyland, and then he'll really be in the woods. He hurries on down the path, forced to follow its circuitous route past the numbered and named and disgraced trees until he's stopped by a chain-link fence. He turns back, intending to march straight out of here. But he's halted at tree eleven, stopped by the blurry mechanical voice coming from the box. He listens. A voice he's already begun to forget speaks to him from the box.

His brother tells him a story he knows well, about a time Marshall's never been able to remember, when he was four and his brother was six. Their mother was outside hanging laundry on the clothesline, and Marshall fell on the basement steps and cut his knee. His brother's voice falters, puzzled. "I guess because we were little, it seemed like she was far away. I couldn't go get her. You were bleeding. I had to be the man in charge. I knew you were supposed to put something on a cut to clean it, so I ran up to the kitchen and got the can of Comet from under the sink and came back and sprinkled it on your cut. It must have stung like hell. Jesus, Marshall, your face when you looked at me."

The tape plays over and over, his brother telling Marshall the same story. Marshall counts 128 words. In the sinking dimness of the coming dusk, Marshall sees the silhouette of his brother cut against an expanse of sky as he stands atop the cliff they've climbed, triumphant.

Debi lives in Mendocino, a coastal California town about the size of Ashland that's been gentrified by tourists and people rich enough to buy second homes, to patronize expensive small restaurants wedged onto the flanks of the coastal mountains. On his first night, Debi wants to take Marshall to one of these restaurants, but he doesn't have the right clothes. His entire wardrobe is packed in his car, and he has nothing but flannel shirts, jeans, and hiking boots to wear. The suit he bought for his brother's funeral — shopping with his parents at Nordstrom the day before the funeral, politely declining the sales clerk's offer to have the suit tailored and ready by the end of the week — hangs in a closet in his parents' house.

Debi calls him "Mountain Man" and fishes from her closet a pair of khaki pants and an oxford shirt that belong to some other man whom she doesn't name. Ordinarily, on principle, he'd refuse to dress for a meal, but somehow he's silenced by the painstaking order of Debi's closet, the carefully gauged comfort of her wood, glass, and tile house, its spaces artfully constructed so that each room on the main floor is open to the others.

She orders for them at the restaurant, and he's quite willing to let her order food he's never heard of—a salad of mesclun, a local wine, stuffed squab, and after dinner, alembic brandy. She makes fun of the pretentious menu, but she orders with the careless familiarity of someone who's been doing this all her life.

It makes him wonder about her. Because she was Kay's roommate, Marshall never thought about Debi much beyond the stability of her company, never felt curious about her the way he did about so many other women. Back then, Marshall thought of Debi as ordinary. She had—still has—a head of tight blond curls, used to study till late every night because she was premed, seemed unafflicted by the compulsion to experiment that preoccupied Marshall's other friends. He doesn't even remember her compact body, so expensively shown off tonight in a black silk dress. As she tells him in her careless, abbreviated way about last winter's trip to Switzerland and her yearly two-week jaunt as a medical volunteer in Central America, he realizes she must have grown up well-off, was probably never so ordinary and self-effacing as he remembers.

When they return to her house, Debi sits out on the deck to smoke, tipping ashes into a metal pail filled with sand.

"I hate the smell of smoke in the house," she says. "I hate for people to find out. I'm a doctor, after all, always riding other people about their bad habits."

"You'd think you'd just quit."

Debi smiles and shrugs.

Marshall had hoped for some answer. It's a dirty habit, one that rightfully ought to accrue shame, secretiveness. "But it's not like you," he says. "It's irrational."

"I'm counting on medical science to keep advancing. By the time I'm old enough to have to pay the piper, maybe a lung transplant will be a piece of cake. Geneticists are already talking about harvesting cells from newborns and cloning them. They can fuse the cell nucleus with an unfertilized egg so they can extract stem cells—cells that haven't yet specialized. They'll be able to refrigerate them for years until you need a new organ. Then they can just grow you a new liver or lung from your own private stock. Maybe we'll all finally have a crack at immortality."

"One-stop organ shopping," Marshall says.

"It's a happy thought," Debi says. "Never having to pay for your mistakes."

It's like her—the woman he remembers—to be so narrow, to think only of what can be anticipated. But this is just one way death can come. There are so many other ways, like the vicious collapse of metal that pierced and crushed his brother's body.

In the quickly descending cold of a coastal night, Marshall shivers in his thin borrowed shirt. "Whose clothes are these?"

She shrugs again. "They've been in my closet for years."

He sleeps that night in her guest room, as well-appointed as a room in a hotel. Swathed in comfort, he sleeps, but he wakes repeatedly to listen to the ticking of a clock, to brush from his cheek a tiny goose down feather that's escaped the pillow, to kick off the bulk of the covers, to list in chronological order the camping trips he took with his brother.

Unlike Isabelle, Debi likes to be in the woods. Every afternoon after she's finished with her patients, they hike together, then return to her house for dinner. When they stop in town for groceries, she doesn't even introduce him to the people who greet her. In the woods, she keeps up with him no matter how rough the terrain, though she pauses for hourly cigarette breaks, sitting on a tree stump, putting out her butts in the dust, and then carefully shredding them into a baggie that she pockets before she gets up to continue their walk. When he camped with his brother, they packed out every last bit of trash they brought in; his brother insisted that they bag even their used toilet paper. Marshall cannot recall anything they talked about on those trips, only feel such longing watching Debi bag her butts that he has to dig his nails into his palms.

He tries to talk to her about Sam. She's a doctor, so she'll understand why he wants to know. He describes his brother's injuries, asks her if Sam could have been saved if the paramedics had gotten him to the hospital sooner. She doesn't think so. With a torn aorta, he would have had massive, rapid blood loss. She can't tell him whether his brother had time to be conscious of pain before he died.

She's as vague when he asks her about some small thing he remembers from their shared past. She merely raises an eyebrow and keeps walking. One afternoon when she puts him off again with, "I didn't know you that well," he takes her by the shoulders, halting her march. He shouts, "Yes you did! Yes you did!"

She pushes him away from her and doesn't speak to him for the rest of the walk. When they get back to her house, she goes to her room and shuts the door. But after he's eaten a solitary dinner, she comes to the kitchen, wearing a bulky terry cloth robe, clutching the collar to her throat.

"Maybe you should go," she says.

When he approaches her, she doesn't flinch. He puts his arms around her. Her body feels so small when it isn't caught and shaped by bra, blouse, nylons. She puts her mouth up to his to kiss him.

So he gets to discover, after all, the different woman she is in bed—his bed, not hers. She nibbles—on his lips when she kisses him, on his skin when she searches hesitantly for the stony outcrop of his nipples on his hairless chest—and her hands too are hesitant, almost reluctant. He is almost rough with her, gripping her hard, plowing through her to get to her, confident that his body will not fail him. Her sighs, when she reaches orgasm, are fluttery and tentative, like her mouth and hands, a fragile answer to the grunts of his pleasure. Afterward they lie in each other's arms to talk. In the darkness, he confesses how hard it is when he visits Kay now, cocooned in her suburban house with two kids, a husband, a dog, content in a way that might have been his to share.

"It's eerie, like looking at my own life through a window," he says. "What could have been."

"No," Debi says. "No. You had no idea how you tormented Kay, did you? All your female best buddies."

"Kay always knew I'd be faithful," Marshall says. "We were always open. It wasn't like that."

"Dream on, Mountain Man," Debi says.

She rolls over, and Marshall doesn't persist. He's sure they'll argue about this again. Now that they are intimate. And all the questions he has about her—whose clothes did she lend him? what secret dissatisfaction with the offerings of the world makes her need to smoke?—still roil inside him, but he can sleep because he knows now the very first secret, the delicacy that skulks inside this small, practical person who covers her refrigerator with neat lists, each anchored by its own tiny magnet. The first secret promises all the rest.

He stays another week, breaking his own schedule for his trip. Each day her reticence fires frustration and ambition in him. He discovers that she talks in her sleep, that she doesn't like to be spoken to until she's had her morning coffee, that she likes to have her curls tugged. Yet he's the one who must nibble at the edges of her, conquer with difficulty the secret of her long-term lover's name—Bob—and feel tantalized by all that she won't confess, by her refusal to take him into her own bed. When it's time for him to leave—she's got to get back to her life, she tells him—they talk about him coming back, trips up and down the coast once he's settled in school.

When he drives over the Golden Gate Bridge, the city of San Francisco is laid out like a vision before him, the hills and houses gilded by late afternoon light, the bay a silvery mirror. Though he's been here before, that first view always seems new to him, gloriously promising. Still, cities make him feel hemmed in. He had to stop over in Point Reyes with his friend Gerard for a few days, gird up for this entrance. He smiles, remembering; Gerard's sister had been visiting at the same time. She and Marshall had gone kayaking while Gerard was at work; they'd weeded the garden together one afternoon, sneaking up to soak each other with the hose and finally tumbling into Gerard's bed. He's begun to expect that no matter where he goes now, some woman will be waiting for him with open arms. It's become so easy that he feels guilty, as if his mysterious power is a form of deceit.

To get to Lee Ann's place, he has to drive through the Haight-Ashbury district, cross Haight Street where the store display windows are still emblazoned with tie-dyed banners, and the kids on the street wear the bell-bottoms and beads of another generation. When he climbs the stairs to her attic apartment in a narrow Victorian, she rushes out to meet him on the landing and embraces him as if he's a prodigal returning home.

They open a celebratory bottle of wine and sit in the two armchairs in her sparsely furnished living room. She apologizes for not having a sofa; her ex-husband took it. There are books stacked on the floor, tenants of a bookcase her husband must also have taken, a few ghostly rectangles on the wall, and only a framed photo of her husband playing the sax on the otherwise naked mantelpiece. Vaguely, Marshall remembers it's been several months since Jeff left her, and he wonders why Lee Ann hasn't replaced the missing pictures or rearranged the remaining furniture.

"You'll have plenty of room to roll out your sleeping bag," Lee Ann says.

When he asks her if she's doing any better, she shrugs and says she'll get over it. She asks about his brother, and he finds it easy to tell her things he's told no one else. He even tells her about hearing Sam's voice in the redwood grove near Crescent City, about stopping in Muir Woods on his way into San Francisco.

"I was going to scatter his ashes there," he says. "We were there together once. But then, so many people go through there every day. It's not the kind of thing you want someone to catch you at."

"I know," Lee Ann says eagerly. "There's this shamefulness to grieving, isn't there?" She stops herself. "You still have his ashes?"

"I was thinking I might find a place near Santa Cruz, in the mountains. Someplace he's never been. I think he'd like that—to go to one more wild place."

For once the tables are turned, and Marshall is the one answering questions, not asking them. He watches Lee Ann, out of a kind of tact, fight the impulse to chime in again with "I know," to make some reference to her husband. He knows all about that anyway, even though he's never met Jeff. Marshall's friendship with Lee Ann is based on a single summer they spent working together, when Lee Ann was temporary staff at the park. But they talked so much that summer. For years they have been writing each other letters that are as open as those conversations, each confiding everything with the haste and fury of someone writing in a diary.

Lee Ann, determined to show him a city good time, takes him out that first night to a jazz bar in North Beach, Pearl's. Absorbed in the music, Lee Ann bites her nails, hunched over, jaw clenched. When they'd worked together, he'd been impressed by her, a working-class girl getting a Ph.D. at Berkeley, all expenses paid. But in spite of her intellectual fierceness, she had annoying habits that marred her attractiveness—nail biting, the frantic flurry of her hands when she talked, her stoop-shouldered modesty. She has changed—this is the first time he's seen her bite her nails on this visit—but still she doesn't seem to know she's nice to look at. This secret she's kept from herself charms him now.

Between sets she talks to Marshall about her teaching. Occasionally she interrupts herself to glance at the door as more people arrive to take in the second set, and he has to call her back to attention. She's passionate about her mission to stir disinterested college freshmen to respond to *The Odyssey, The Aeneid,*

The Epic of Gilgamesh, all the ancient, immortal epics. She tells her students that these are riches and that the world is conspiring to keep these riches from them, sandblasting them with titillating consumer longing and the wish fulfillment of movies. Marshall finds this archaic but beautiful, like the old, elegant philosophical proofs of the immateriality of the soul, so inadvertently and easily shattered by the progress of science, the reduction of thought to a finite chemical reaction.

They stay till the second set is finished, and then at 2:00 A.M. they head across the street to the Vesuvio Cafe, with its colored mosaic glass windows, where again Lee Ann scans the room as if she's looking for someone. They take a table by the window and sit over bowl-sized cups of coffee, and Marshall wonders at her—doesn't she have to get up in the morning to teach?—but Lee Ann says she got used to staying out late and getting up early when she was with Jeff, who kept a musician's hours.

When they get back to her apartment, Lee Ann says she has only three hours before she has to go to class anyway, so she makes more coffee and they sit on the floor together—it is impossible to feel close sitting in those two winged armchairs—and talk about how neither of them can sleep. It confuses him to talk about this with Lee Ann when he's so clear—has been lifted into such an architecturally open sense of time—and she's so muddy. She thinks she ought to burn the few things Jeff left behind; she can't sleep unless she's clutching an old shirt, unwashed, that he left in the hamper.

It's so easy to hold her in his arms. Lee Ann leans against him and cries, and he makes a soothing sound and runs his hand over her hair, again and again. Her dark hair is the color of Isabelle's, he thinks, but Lee Ann cries and cries, and then he's uncertain about the similarity. His mouth glances against Lee Ann's cheek.

She pushes him away, wrapping her arms around herself, making herself ugly. "God, I can't stand it."

"He's not dead," Marshall says.

Lee Ann apologizes immediately, accepts so humbly this cruelty that leaves Marshall shocked at himself. What's the matter with him? He reaches for her. But she scrambles to her feet, escapes him. She goes to take a long shower, and when she comes back, she says resolutely, "Let's have fun while you're here."

During the day while she's teaching, Marshall goes to the art museums or walks at Land's End, following the path from the cypress-studded cliffs west of the Golden Gate Bridge to the city's west coast until, past the Cliff House, he hikes down to Ocean Beach and walks for miles. Once Lee Ann takes him to class with her, and he watches her charm her students with her peculiar combination of conviction and self-doubt. She rips into a recent translation of Homer for its dull language, then looks up to plead with her students: "Do you see what I mean?"

Nearly every night they go out to hear jazz, at Pearl's or another club where local bands play. After four ragged, joyful nights, Lee Ann offers Marshall one of her sleeping pills. Before she takes one for herself, she counts the precious remaining few. When she lets him into her bed, she curls her body into a tight fist, but he is determined to get over that barrier. He kneads the bunched muscles of her shoulders, confident that she will become pliant under his touch, his gift for abundance. She pushes him away. He cannot understand her stubborn refusal to be absolved.

They're at Pearl's again when Lee Ann, habitually glancing up to see who's in the room, halts in midsentence and gets up from the table. She steps up behind a man who's still busy paying his cover charge to the woman at the door and waits for him to notice her. Marshall feels a twinge of jealousy. The man has to be her husband. For him, Lee Ann's face collapses slowly, like a clay hillside giving way in a hard rain. Marshall doesn't want to look at that either, so why does he feel such a surge of anger when the man finally notices Lee Ann and flinches?

Marshall is on his feet and beside the guy in an instant. He shoves Jeff on the shoulder, forcing him to take a step back to keep from being knocked off his feet.

"Leave her alone!" Marshall shouts. "Leave her alone!"

Lee Ann stares as if she doesn't know him or see him. Marshall tugs her, feels her jacket bunch reassuringly in his hand, yanks until her feet move, and drags her out of the bar. She's like a flimsy packet of matches beneath the bunched cloth that fills his fist, so light, so easy to keep pushing ahead of him.

Out on the street, the sickly smell of car exhaust, stale urine, and greasy food assaults him. He's stayed here too long, exceeded his tolerance for the claustrophobic compactness of city sounds and smells. He wishes he'd stayed with Debi in her glass house above the ocean, with the horizon that stretched endlessly beyond the window.

Lee Ann twists abruptly, pushes into his braced arm, into his chest. She struggles to go back. When he steps forward, she's become a heaviness that he can't wade through, a wall of stone.

Her mouth moves against his skin. "It's crazy." She pants for breath, as if she's the one who had to keep pushing. "To hope for something as much as you dread it."

Even her voice sounds unfamiliar to him, tinny, metallic, like the faded recording of his brother's voice trying to speak to him from far away, from forever.

They make slow progress along the crowded sidewalk. Marshall can't remember where he parked his car on these narrow, winding streets. He wants to keep going, leave Lee Ann behind. But he has to go back to her apartment, where he's left his sleeping bag, his shaving kit, his clothes, the tin canister containing his brother. A few ounces of dust, a few pathways between neurons in Marshall's brain that will dwindle with disuse.

Marshall's senses greedily inform him of the warmth of Lee Ann pressed against him, but their brutally imperfect span cannot encompass anything so immaterial as her futile wishes. Oh God, he doesn't want to be trapped here.

written in stone

Hassan comes to me on Tuesday nights. He is having more difficulty than I am with our separation. I don't know how other people manage to cancel one another out of their lives. I can't. He can't. Hassan can't do anything by half-measures; he won't be reassured that we remain friends unless I see him every week.

He lets himself in—he still has a key—while I am at the gym, and by the time I get home, I can smell lamb in the oven, and the sauce, *khoresht*, bubbling away on the stove, seeping the scent of cinnamon and garlic and stewed cherries. The Persian rice steams over a low flame, a dishcloth laid under the lid of the pot, part of the process of fussing over it that doesn't seem to account for the spectacular results, flaky rice that forms a crunchy golden crust on the bottom.

We kiss. I take off my jacket and go to the sink to wash lettuce for salad. He says I don't have to help, I look tired, but I insist that I'm fine. Hassan watches me anxiously. He expects to read in my body some distressing proof of injury—circles under the eyes, stooped shoulders, the abrupt collapse of muscles that will make me literally an old woman, a thrown-away woman. I'm forty-six, and I go to the gym five days a week, and I've told him he can forget it, I'm not going to make it that easy for him.

I tell him about the new orthopedic surgeon at the hospital; the guy seems OK, only he plays country-and-western music during surgery. Hassan is quick to see this as domineering. Surgeons are as cocky as fighter pilots, but they bear the entire burden of risk; no one has yet sued me for handing a surgeon the wrong piece of gauze. I shrug. "Maybe he just has bad taste in music."

When we talk about Hassan's job, we're talking about the problems of the entire world. Somehow, with a degree in structural engineering, Hassan ended up working for a nonprofit here in San Francisco that arranges conferences between government officials and scientists and businesspeople from all over the globe. He pursues the world's grievances without any of the pessimism his country's history should have instilled in him. And he happens to be awfully good at parties and getting people interested in one another. He has three hundred names in his E-mail address book. He loves every person on that list, from his colleagues to the security guy in his building to the earnest minor bureaucrats from Uruguay and Indonesia.

Hassan complains to me about his job, which he never used to do. Sometimes I wonder if he means to console me—he may have left me for another, but he is not perfectly happy—but then he'd started complaining before he left.

"Now that we're respectable, everyone becomes cautious," Hassan says. "I am not supposed to enjoy myself so much at the cocktail parties and banquets. What does this mean? What's too much enjoyment?"

He met this woman when she performed at some benefit. I don't know if he decided to love her in particular or if, out of innocence and boldness, she forced his hand by taking literally his long-standing and general offer to the world.

My husband—my soon to be ex-husband?—is a warm and affectionate man, a nostalgic creature. When we went back to Iran, we lived under one roof with his entire family. The man badgered his mother to teach him to make all the foods he'd missed when he was at college in the U.S. He and I were happy—very happy—for twenty years. He brought me tulips on every anniversary. I always knew where he had left his reading glasses. He used to save the notes I left under his coffee cup every morning when I left for work, stuff the scraps of paper in the top drawer of his dresser, where they accumulated until he moved out. Hassan is in a predicament, all right.

Hassan turns the rice out of the pot, shapes it into a perfect cone, and makes an impression into which he ladles the lamb and the *khoresht*. We eat by candlelight—something we had forgotten to do anymore when we lived together—and Hassan works steadily at a bottle of red wine.

He slips toward her; he can't help it. He's tired, he says, because she didn't sleep last night. She works late, is used to staying up late. When he first told me about her, so proud to announce she was a singer, I almost burst out laughing. The wife—suited up every day in surgical scrubs, paper cap hiding my frosted hair, plastic booties over my orthopedic shoes, so de-sexed you can tell my gender only by the size of my bones. The lover—a sultry chanteuse.

Hassan tells me he has discovered that Monica is an insomniac. "She stays up, then she feels blue, and then she can't stand it, so she brings a bottle of brandy back to bed and wakes me up to talk."

It could be too that this is her way of testing him. She must have plenty of younger men available to her. "Maybe she has to find out if you can keep up."

"Do you know," Hassan says, "how old and slow she makes me feel? If it's any comfort."

This is his way of testing me, the limits of my tolerance. "I don't feel that way," I say. "It's not like that for me at all."

"I won't talk about her if it bothers you."

Why does everyone expect me to be bitter? I've been avoiding my girlfriends, who want to take me out on Saturdays, who seem to think it's going to save my life to sit in a bar with them and consider the forms of torture appropriate to husbands who take up with younger women.

"No," I say. "I'm interested."

He wonders how she manages for so long on so little sleep. She has to get up and go to work in the mornings too, boring temp jobs to pay the rent, at least until she can earn steady money as a singer, graduate from wedding gigs to a local opera company. Then he tells me what else he's just discovered about her.

"She has some kind of dyslexia when it comes to directions," he says. "The other night I let her drive home from a party, and I fell asleep in the car. She had to wake me up in order to find the way to her own house. She can't tell left from right. She finds her way by memorizing landmarks, only she has a harder time at night, and if she strays from her route, she has no idea where she is."

Hassan embroiders the moment until the dyslexia becomes some touching spiritual dislocation, a signifying vulnerability.

He didn't fall asleep. He passed out. I worry about him without me. I never drink as much as he does and can always get him home.

Hassan's stories of his courtship—the trouble he takes to elaborate—remind me of the traditional Persian dances he and his friends used to perform when we were all in college. All of the Persians were studying engineering or computer science or medicine, things that would be useful to the Shah's technological society. They shared apartments, they kissed each other, they cooked together. They paired off to dance to tapes they'd brought with them from Iran. One of them would take the role of the woman and make everyone laugh at the exaggerated sinuousness of his rolling hips and unfurling arms, his pursed lips. Their tradition codified this lasciviousness, cleared a space for it, a secret out in the open.

Hassan and I went back to Iran in 1977, after we graduated from college. Hassan's mother had been widowed the year before, and he felt a duty to return to his family, to repay his country for his education. We'd just gotten married. There's the story of what happened to us in those years in Iran—Hassan tells it better than I could—and then there are those vivid memories that continue to live in me like sensation, not recollected but reborn whenever they are aroused. I can still return to the garden of his mother's house, an inner courtyard walled in by overgrown pink climbing roses, their branches so thick and luxuriant that anyone who dared their thorns could be hidden entirely beneath their leaves. A path of stones wound through salvia and fanning clusters of white lilies. In a shady corner a flowering vine shaped itself in fluid arabesques in its drive for light. The English word *paradise* comes from the Persian word for an enclosed garden, *pairi-daeza*.

On Ashura, the tenth day of Muharram, I watched from the window as men marched past the house, their wailing echoing off the walls of the buildings that faced the narrow street. They lashed themselves with chains and belts, scoring the skin of their bare backs. Some of them flinched when they drew blood; others did not waver in their intoxicated chanting. Their faces were not hungry but hard with satisfaction. Hassan was in such a hurry to explain. These men were commemorating the death of Hossein, their long-ago martyr, and this was their atonement, their allotment of his sacrifice. Hassan shrugged. They had so little else. This was just the sort of thing that the West sensationalized; I mustn't make that mistake. When I *did* see what was before my eyes: how real God is to the poor.

The Shah's regime was already crumbling, with all the randomly intensified dangers of collapse; the mullahs had grown intransigent; Hassan's sister had taken to wearing a head scarf so she wouldn't be harassed in the street; her brothers debated how this concession might be understood politically; and their mother remembered how the Shah's father had forced women to give up the chador. The world might begin to move at a raging pace, with the moan and roar of those men in the street, and still one lives a slower life in private, stubborn and tentative and intricate in its flourishing. I'd sneak out to that garden to enjoy the relief of being alone, to savor all that I was learning about my husband's family—Hassan and his two brothers, cracking pistachio nuts between their fingers, arguing with the same vivid energy of the boys I'd known in the U.S.; his mother snipping roses and dropping them in a bucket, smiling and nodding to supplement the Farsi words I did not understand.

I cook this time, so it's simple: steak, baked potatoes, peas. I stand all day at work. I sterilize slender implements and lay them out in exacting order on a paper-sheeted tray. In an orthopedic surgical unit, every gesture, like the implements, is scaled to the miniature—the surgeon slices a precisely calibrated seam through tissue, scrapes away at bone in increments that will minimize nerve damage, or studies a video screen that projects images captured by a camera lens so small it can be threaded into the body. I don't want to come home to core or peel or dice or fillet.

Hassan is in trouble from another quarter. He has wooed a little too zealously the representative of a foundation that might fund his organization.

He takes both my hands in his to plead his case. "We went out for drinks. We're relaxing, I think. And the next day she calls my boss and says she's uncomfortable dealing with me. I've sexualized the interaction."

Another time, his need to befriend a fund-raiser might yield a grant, or he might take a guest from India to a drag show and delight him instead of shock him. More than once he's gotten conference delegates drunk in order to soften their attitudes toward one another. If it doesn't work out, he is undaunted. He'd roll the dice again if he had to, and let someone else hold his breath. No one wrote to tell him when his mother got sick, for fear he'd rush back to Iran. His brother waited to tell Hassan until it was too late for him to come to the funeral. Maybe it was safe for Hassan to return, maybe he could have visited years ago, and only superstition made us believe that history was written in stone.

Hassan frowns. "I think I touched her elbow. A couple of times."

And probably he pressed too close, the way he must lean across the table now in order to talk, really talk, to me. Persians routinely invade what an American would consider inviolate personal space. Hassan is so Americanized now, and yet these essential habits persist.

"Would it do any good to call her and apologize?" I say.

"I am forbidden to contact her. Forbidden."

"Do they understand at work that she just misread you?"

"They say, 'Don't drink. Don't drink on the job.'"

He did stop drinking for a few months last year, after he learned that his mother had died. He didn't decide to quit; he just lost interest for a while, the way he lost interest in everything else. Maybe they should have written him that his mother was ill. Hassan hadn't seen her for twenty years, not since we left Iran.

Hassan strokes my hands. "With this woman—I thought we were sympathetic, that's all. Remember the good old days, when we were so delighted by the freedom to be sexual? Now we must hide it. We must behave like automatons in our professional lives."

I smile. "Nobody has any fun anymore."

"Exactly," Hassan says. He smiles at me. "Are you? Having any fun?"

"What?"

"Dating someone."

"Don't feel up to it yet."

"What about that new doctor? You have such expressive eyes. Why don't you give him a come-hither look the next time you're handing him a scalpel or changing a CD for him? What if he wants you already? 'Nurse, oh nurse, I have an itch. Can you scratch it for me?'"

"What happened? Did you and your girl have a fight?"

"She's not a girl. We're going to drive up to Tahoe this weekend and go skiing. She's going to teach me."

"I'll be seeing you in the ortho unit on Monday."

"Don't be silly. I'm staying on the bunny hill. I'm planning to fall down a lot. It must be very safe to fall down in the snow. She will have to come and help me up every time. She'll fall in love with me a thousand times more."

A thousand times he'd flirted, a thousand times been taken too seriously, and then he brought these interesting people home to introduce them to me. He didn't bring her home, though he kept talking about her. I made him leave. I didn't want to beg. I still remember the hurt, stunned look on his face when I told him to go.

"It's true that we fight," Hassan says. "But the fights—they're very good, actually. Big scenes."

Ever since we lived in Iran, I've been afraid for Hassan, the way you are afraid ever after for a child who's long since recovered from some serious illness. I never want to be as afraid again as I was during those two years. He'd found work right away, consulting with construction crews who were building the roads and bridges and office towers of the Shah's future, and he was popular with the crews. He told jokes; he brought pastries to the site; he had some story about a goat crossing a bridge that was meant to illustrate the principles of weight distribution. He shrugged when bribes had to be paid. And then he was taken in for questioning. He'd told a joke that everyone was telling: the Shah makes a phone call to hell, and when he asks the operator for the charges, he is told there aren't any, it's a local call. Hassan was picked up by the secret police at a job site, and one of the foremen risked his own neck by sending a worker to the house to tell us.

We were not sure where Hassan had been taken. His oldest brother made a few hopeless phone calls, and then we waited. We sat in the living room on chairs covered with crocheted doilies. Later that afternoon Hassan walked in the door with his jacket over his arm, his shirt soaked through with sweat. He had to work a little this time at being himself. "Nothing to worry about," he said. He had only been questioned for a few hours; the SAVAK men had let him off easy. His mother cried, and he promised her he would be careful; he'd tell a different joke the next time.

I was afraid whenever he left the house after that. I never ran into trouble on the street; I dyed my hair brown and wore a scarf like Hassan's sister, gave shots at the clinic where I'd found useful work, and stopped trying to make conversation with the patients. But Hassan could not choose to be careful. Some urge in him that he couldn't repress would prompt him to make up a story about materials disappearing daily from the job site, or burst out singing some American rock song, or flare up when his instructions for placing rebar hadn't been followed to the letter.

Any of these things could have sealed his fate, and that didn't change when the revolution came, relatively bloodless but not peaceful. Hassan greeted the revolution with anticipation—from such ardor anything might flow. He could no longer find work as an engineer, but he could teach math to high school students. Only he could not help sympathizing with faculty who were denounced by their students. He would not relinquish the necktie he so hated, because someone wished to make him. He would not give up visiting friends in the evening, even though the guards at the checkpoints on the road beat anyone they suspected of drinking. He chewed parsley to disguise the smell of liquor on his breath.

The frenzy would die down soon, Hassan said. Ayatollah Khomeini loved the Sufi poet Rumi, had written poems himself as a younger man. When the *komitehs* began to appear and issue their own laws over their neighborhood fiefdoms, because the revolution had succeeded so far in advance of its ability to govern, Hassan was the one who stood in line to get permission to buy food, fluid at the task of bartering, teasing, and cajoling the armed young men who wanted not bribes but a tithe for the mullahs. He'd joke, to *them*, that the cost of living hadn't changed a bit.

Hassan's sister left the country, smuggling out jewelry as insurance not just for herself but for the rest of the family. His family wanted Hassan to go next. But Persians prefer not to confront one another. They chose intermediaries—an aunt, an uncle—to hint at this. Without result. I felt as if my nerves had been soaked in some flammable solution, priming me forever for dread. I burst into tears one day when Hassan came home from the market on time, as promised. Hassan applied for an exit visa a week later, but he was refused. Finally we left illegally, crossing the border into Turkey on foot, like refugees. From there we returned to America, a place where his impulsiveness would not cost him his life.

Hassan cancels on the next Tuesday but comes the following week. I arrive after he does. I don't want to sit and wait for him. He serves me *dolmeh*, rice flecked with the golden bits of crust and sprinkled with saffron threads, and duck baked with pomegranates and basted with their juice. He has brought a bottle of vodka this time, instead of a bottle of wine, and he fills two tumblers full. If I didn't know better, I'd accuse Hassan of courting me.

"Why are we getting drunk?" I ask.

"You know I like vodka," he says. "And I have to celebrate. I believe I've been demoted again."

"Why?"

"They're claiming we've raised enough money to hire someone whose job it is to raise money, so I can concentrate on event plan-

ning. They put it very nicely." He sighs. "I must have said something to that woman that I can't remember."

"I had no idea they were so Puritan."

"It's inevitable," Hassan says. "It's been coming for a long time."

"Don't be too unhappy."

He smiles at me. "They're taking away from me the part of my
job that I hate the most. Really, I *should* celebrate. Life is good. We
have a plan afoot to hold regional conferences, and this would be
a great thing. Give little countries a chance to solve their problems
for themselves. Oh! And I didn't break any bones when we went
skiing."

"Why do you have to tempt fate?"

"It was an adventure. And did I tell you I am going to be on the
stage? Monica and I are going to be extras in the opera. She gets
to sing a few lines. I get to stand at the back and hold a spear."

He's still slender, and he has the kind of dark, striking looks that
come across well on stage. There's a reason so many women have
misread his intentions.

"Will you come to see me?" Hassan asks.

"No. I'd like to see you, but I'll pass on seeing her."

He looks stricken.

"I just don't want to have to set eyes on her and discover she's
a luscious young thing. I'd rather think of her as nothing special.
Kind of dumpy."

"Will you feel better if I tell you things are not perfect with us?"

"She's not dumpy, is she?"

"Because she's mad at me. I'm in the doghouse. I banged up
the car on the way home from a planning meeting last week. I hit
a pole when I was backing out of a parking spot, and that doesn't
even really count. But now she's thinking I'm drinking too much,
that's the reason. I ask her if she wants to sign on as a consultant
to my boss, she throws things. My God, she throws my shoes out
the window, so I'll have to go downstairs to get them and she can
lock me out. It's terrible."

"That's why you brought the vodka."

"If it's good vodka," he says, "no one can smell it on your breath."

"Isn't this a case of the pot calling the kettle black? Didn't you tell me she drags a bottle of brandy to bed and wakes you up in the middle of the night?"

"But you see, this is the rub. She threw out the last of her very good brandy. She wants to prove to me that this is important to her. She will do anything for me. She will quit drinking with me."

"Now *that* I didn't expect," I say. "I thought she was supposed to be so arty."

"I know. But no. She is strict. So, all right, I say to myself, this would be a sacrifice. But then I want to know, what could be on the other side of that? What would it be like? Do you think I should quit? Maybe I should try it."

Hassan pours himself another tumbler of vodka. "So. We toast. Here's to our friends and well-wishers. Here's to my last glass of vodka."

We clink glasses.

"Also," he says. "She turns out to be jealous. She wants to know why I have to come and have dinner with you."

What story of me does he tell her, of all that binds us, without intending this consequence?

"Tell her I'm being a harridan about money," I say. "That way she won't worry."

If I didn't see him every week, I wouldn't know if he had dinged a post or found a new crusade at work or fallen asleep at the wheel and awakened just in time.

Our first years back in the U.S., we worried all the time about Hassan's family in Iran. His middle brother got out, but Hassan's mother refused to leave, and so his oldest brother stayed with her. There was the hostage crisis, the gas shortage, the embargo; we had to contrive ways to get money to Hassan's family, all illegal.

Hassan's sister came out to us from New York, where she'd first gone; she'd married and had a little boy and gotten divorced in short order, another worry. Hassan had difficulty finding work as an engineer—we persuaded ourselves it was the recession—and he didn't like the work when he got it. Someone threw a cup of coffee at him one morning when he was in a long line at the gas station. He wouldn't have told me except that he ruined his sport coat trying to wash out the stain himself. "Well," he said, "he called me a dirty Arab, and I decided it wasn't a good time to inform him that I was Iranian, and Iranians are not Arabs."

None of this could keep us from being happy. We lived carefully so Hassan could send money home, but we always had enough for little trips. We went away at least once a month, even if it was only to a friend's cabin in Inverness. We enjoyed having our nephew in the house, making forts out of sofa cushions and filling the house with balloons for his birthday, and it was only a favor, not a duty, to give up a concert or a party when his mother needed us to watch him. I never agonized about the value of my work the way Hassan did; I was already doing enough living after hours. We had huge, raucous parties. We invited Hassan's fellow exiles, people he'd met at some futile political committee or on a construction site, a couple of nurses, teachers, his sister's friends from graduate school. If people weren't dancing, they were arguing fiercely, and Hassan would be in the middle of them, usually standing, wavering on his feet. He would tease and cajole and browbeat his friends in his desire for agreement. They must not complain so bitterly about Reagan; his election was necessary to the survival of the left in America, just as the frenzy in Iran was every day making possible the triumph of democracy and reason. I never argued; I plied people with food and drink and smiled a lot. I was a bleached blonde then, with a collection of beaded and silky dresses I wore for these parties, and I enjoyed the dismay and suspicion of some of Hassan's friends, their assumption that the marriage must be about sex. I wanted them to think that.

Once, for a Fourth of July party, Hassan smuggled in some fireworks from Oregon, and he set them off in the backyard of our rented house, surrounded by an audience, of course. One of the Roman candles misfired and shot into the pine tree that shaded the yard. The tree ignited like a torch, its trunk becoming a slender column of flame. Someone called the fire department; I hid what was left of the fireworks; and Hassan got the hose and doused the fire. We should have been arrested, but Hassan convinced the firefighters that a spark from the barbecue had ignited the tree. Hours later, after everyone had gone home, I was still nervous that a spark might reignite in that dry Monterey pine. So Hassan and I kept vigil in the yard, wrapped in blankets, looking up through the blackened branches at the stars. In his arms, I fell asleep to the sound of the pinecones in the tree snapping and crackling, releasing the residual heat and energy of the fire.

Hassan cancels on me two Tuesdays in a row. When he calls the next Tuesday afternoon, to cancel again, I tell him I don't want to hear another made-up excuse. He doesn't have to torture me; he can just say that he won't be coming anymore.

"No, no, no," he says, "that's not it." He is silent for a moment. "I stopped drinking. Pretty much. I am supposed to go to the AA meeting on Tuesday night."

"That's where you've been?"

"No, no. Tonight is the first time. This is a condition—a big condition—she sets for me. I don't know about this. I'm not very good at organized activities."

"Where is this meeting? I could meet you when it's over, and we could go for pizza."

"Would you?" he says. "Would you come in with me, just this first time?"

"Isn't that against the rules?"

"If we have to, we will come up with a story for you to confess too."

I consider staying home alone. I've been trying to break that habit. I've been dating a guy I met at work, a medical-instrument salesman who sat in on surgery to demonstrate a new arthroscope. We've gone out for two Saturdays in a row. We kissed on the second date, a chaste, closed-mouth kiss.

"Give me the address."

Hassan is waiting for me outside the church social room. When we go inside, the meeting is already underway, so we find seats in the back. People take turns going to the front of the room to announce that they are alcoholics. Some of them describe their most recent temptation, others tell stories of the way that alcohol has rotted their lives. A man does not know how to begin to beg his children for forgiveness. A woman describes how she followed the AA formula for resisting temptation: she stopped to register her emotion, unburdened herself of her anger, got a good night's sleep, made sure she ate a hearty breakfast. Hassan whispers in my ear, "She looks like she eats a hearty breakfast." After a few more minutes, he nudges me again. "Why does everybody discover that they drink for the exact same reasons? Why do you have to go to bed at exactly 10 P.M. to stay sober?"

I giggle. He snickers. The urge to laugh becomes so strong that it's like a spasm. Soon both of us are shaking with the effort to stifle our laughter.

We beat a hasty retreat, shutting the door quietly behind us, and once we are outside, we yield to the irresistible impulse to hoot and howl.

We sit on the back bumper of my car while we decide where to go. Hassan says he would really like a drink. He holds out his hand, level and steady. "I am not shaking or anything. So I cannot be addicted. Which means I *can* have a drink."

He sits so that his shoulder touches mine. "This AA," he says. "This indoctrination. I can't stomach it."

I wonder if he is even conscious of his mania for contact. When I closed my eyes to kiss that salesman, I felt careful, vigilant, the way I am in surgery, where it's my job, not the surgeon's, to pre-serve the sterile field. "You don't have to come to these meetings," I say. "You don't even have to quit drinking."

"I just jumped off that cliff—sure, sure, I would promise this woman the moon, and they'll stop nagging me at work into the bargain. What did I do this for? I must be a crazy alcoholic. I act like one."

He takes my hand, and my fingers grip his instinctively.

I am so intently focused on his hand in mine that it hurts. As if I'm a new wife, not one accustomed to this habit.

Hassan kicks at the bumper of the car. "You know, she doesn't eat, all day. So many opera singers are fat; maybe it's an edge for her if she can starve herself. And I hate this in her."

My patience, my forbearance, has finally been rewarded. I am a new wife. I am again stealing off to the garden to indulge my delirium. Here are the roses, the salvia, the vine that cunningly, effortlessly routes its growth toward the light.

"I can't stop myself from trying to tempt her," Hassan says. "Eat, eat, eat! It's myself I'm trying to encourage. I'm not so greedy as I thought."

I did not worry when Hassan curled up into a silent mourning after his mother died. It was in his nature. No half-measures. He reread all her letters, thin onionskin pages saved for years in a fat manila envelope. One night I sat with him while he read. He said, "We should have had children." He never said it to me again. He didn't really mean it. He was grieving.

Hassan makes a sound that is not quite a laugh, not quite a moan. "Why have I done this to you? Behaving like an idiot! And what for?"

He lifts an arm, but something catches at the gesture, and he lets his hand drop heavily in his lap.

When I want him to flow like water over stone.

I watch his face for a moment. I begin the story for him. I tell him, "You fell in love."

He seems to gather himself. And then he's off. "It's terrible, this kind of love. Always butting heads. Always struggling."

I let him lean against me. Soon all those AA people will come out of their meeting and give us dirty looks. I've been afraid too long to register so small a threat. Only I didn't know enough to be frightened all those years ago, when those men were marching in the street, flogging their bodies, driving themselves forward.

behold
the handmaid
of the lord

I cannot match what my hands are doing to any intention until I look in the mirror. When I look there, I meet my client's eyes and we talk at each other's reflection. Should the layers blend more gradually? Should we take more off at the sides? I check the mirror again when I drag my fanned fingers through her hair to see how it falls. In one realm, my job is piecemeal, merely manual labor, snipping the difficult material of wet hair, tugging a comb through tangles, rolling strands of hair over a brush to blow-dry it, and in the other realm, these parts are so strangely merged into our mutual anticipation. When she gets up from the chair, we'll pretend it hasn't happened, this conspiracy of unreasonable wishes. A lot of my clients don't even recognize me when I see them on the street.

After I finish with my client, I sit in the chair and wait for Molly to finish her last customer of the day so she can color my hair. So many times I've fixed people up for weddings, retirement parties, awards banquets, and tomorrow it's my turn.

Anyone can write in to get on the Family Secrets segment of Vivian Woods's talk show. I used to believe they staged all of it—the man who screamed at his wife when she told him their youngest child wasn't his, the sister who forgave her brother for stealing from her when he was on drugs. The spectacle was just as thrilling whether someone flew into a fury or burst into tears. Then I saw this teenage girl on there. She said her parents got divorced when she was twelve. She and her mother were always fighting, and she wanted to live with her father. One day her mother slapped her, and the girl dug her fingers into her arm till she had a bruise she could show her teacher. Child Protective Services came to evaluate her mother, and the girl got to go and live with her father.

Her mother's face was projected on a video screen behind the girl, because they always sequester the surprised party in a booth offstage—I guess the show's producers worry about getting sued if an actual fistfight breaks out. The girl had to repeat the story she'd told the audience. And there was her mother crying on the video screen, and I started to cry. They were both hurting so much, together. The girl kept begging her, but the mother said she couldn't forgive her. It was real.

My secret would be run-of-the-mill if the man I'd slept with hadn't been my cousin's fiancé. She's gotten over the breakup with Peter, finally married a nice guy, has a kid. She's happy now, like she deserves to be. Anna Marie pulls me next to her for pictures at family picnics and wonders why I don't want to go out on Fridays with her and Roger, when I might meet someone, and it's been so long. I've been spoiled by what happened with Peter, by what I was willing to do to have him.

My client comes back with a tip, a dollar bill folded up small as shame in her hand. At the better salons, customers leave tips in a tiny envelope and write your name on it, but here at SuperShears we still press palms when we take our tips.

Molly waltzes over and whips a plastic poncho over my shoulders. We debate whether to use bleach or a gentler tint to highlight my hair. Molly says the bleach will be too brassy and chooses a honey-colored tint. "You want soft highlights, like Princess Di had."

"Let's not get carried away," I say. But the wish rises in me like fish to the bait.

"You don't want to look like a slut," Molly says. "Even if you acted like one."

Princess Di had that trick of tucking her chin and looking up at people, at the camera, so that in all the pictures her eyes look wide and innocent. Look what she did, fooling around with her bodyguard, and she's still the world's darling, even dead.

Molly gives me a slap on the shoulder to remind me to laugh. I don't know why I told her, when I have told no one else for four years, when we're not that close. She teases me about it the way she teases me about the way I lay out my station every morning, lining up my tools in specific order, rinsing the combs twice in sterilizing solution. *Why all the fuss?* She says she has her own married man or two—*but he wasn't married,* I say, and she says, *same difference*—and what you've got to realize is you're a chump if you fall for one of them.

Molly puts on plastic gloves and begins separating strands of my hair. She paints them with coloring solution and wraps them in foil. The smell of the solution is as disturbing as the intimate smells of a body, the sweet, almost fruity smell of Peter's sweaty crotch, the faintly metallic odor of his armpits, the astonishing sourness of digestion on his breath. These are secrets I have no right to know about Anna Marie.

"Well, you've inspired me," Molly says. "I've always wanted to get on Letterman. With my stupid dog trick. When I play the recorder, my dog howls along—in key! I figure if you can get on TV for something like this, I've got a chance."

"This isn't for fun," I say.

"Sure. Beneath that quiet exterior, you're just an exhibitionist at heart."

When the letter came from Vivian Woods's producer, I was scared—how could I do this to Anna Marie?—and I kept taking the letter from its envelope to reread it, to feel the thick, expensive paper. On my Mondays off I've watched plenty of people tell their story to Vivian Woods and Oprah Winfrey and Sally Jessie Raphael. Their own story shakes each of them furiously in its teeth, a last chance far more potent than Oprah nodding her head or Sally rolling her eyes or Vivian scolding.

Molly leans down and puts her face close to mine. "How on earth did you talk your cousin into this?"

It's all I can do not to flinch at this breach of safe distance. I won't ride crowded buses or stay in line if people step close enough to brush against me, and I always stand behind the client in the chair. But still I didn't see it coming, that day in the grocery store. I was reaching for apples to put in a plastic bag, and the man just sneaked a hand under my arm and squeezed my breast. He was gone before I could clutch my arms to my chest. I found a clerk, a teenage boy. I was shaking and yelling, and the clerk looked at me like I was the one who'd done something.

"Anna Marie's going to hate me," I say. I hadn't gotten up the nerve yet to ask her to go on TV when that man grabbed me. He knew. Even the clerk staring at me knew, had scented it on me, or seen it in me, that openness to violation that doesn't distinguish who's on which end of the kick.

"Then you should have let sleeping dogs lie," Molly says.

My mother always said this when we had to smuggle some wish past my father. When I was a kid, I even thought of him as a dog, a big muscled mastiff stretched out in his armchair, his fury a thing we could escape if we tiptoed around him. If I wanted new clothes or money to go on a Girl Scout trip or permission to go to my first dance, we maneuvered, and he remained still as the axis of the planet.

My mother worried about me her last few years because I never brought home a boyfriend. She worried as if there were only a slender chance that I might get lucky and slip past the fanged dog that stood between us and all our wishes. I couldn't help feeling relief last year when she died: she won't ever know. She'd never say *slut*. She'd say *whore*. Some strange kind of creature that she wouldn't recognize if she saw it in the flesh.

"It's the guilt," I say. "I can't keep living with it."

Molly snorts. "Don't give me that Catholic line of bull. You can cure obsessive thinking if you want to. That's how I quit smoking. I went to this therapy group, and they taught us how to change our thinking patterns. See, whenever you want a cigarette, really crave one, you're supposed to visualize this red stop sign in your head. And you can't go past it. Your thoughts have to stop right there. It works."

Molly tugs at another strand of my hair, and I let my head bob under her hand. This could hypnotize you, this rhythmic touch. Usually I do my own hair and so am deprived of the luxury of having my body ministered to by another. The body's pleasures all pool in one place, and Molly's gentle tugs sink there to become Peter's hands, touching me, coaxing me. I can't stop this any more than I can stop the sick feeling I get when I think of Anna Marie. I see myself, my own body in its intricate connections to Peter's, as if I stood to the side and watched while we were together. I am sitting cross-legged on my bed, naked, and his fingers are tracing in order every knot of bone along my spine, reading this code. Sometimes when I am alone on an elevator, I will press my fingers to the bumps of Braille lettering beside the buttons for each floor, and just like now, when Molly's tug recalls for me the liquid possibilities of my spine, I'll be under Peter's hands again, miraculously being taught the word that my body is, the pleading speech.

I couldn't get out of flying down to Los Angeles with Anna Marie. We sit stuffed into our economy-class seats, and Anna Marie pulls down the tray so she can empty her old wallet into the new wallet she's just bought. She's pleased to have a chore she can cross off her list while we're flying.

"Maybe this afternoon, after the show, we can go out to lunch," Anna Marie says. "Window-shop on Rodeo Drive, just like the ladies of the manor."

I'd hoped they'd fly us down the night before, put us up in hotel rooms, sequester me from Anna Marie, but the shuttle flight from San Francisco takes only an hour, and Vivian Woods's operation is run economically. Anna Marie naturally wanted to travel together—she's always apologizing to me because she doesn't have as much time for me as she used to before she had Eli. She thinks it's her fault we don't see each other so much anymore. What I imagine will happen after I tell her is a kind of gray wash, vague and obscuring as fog, but I know there won't be any giggling shopping trip this afternoon.

She sighs. "I wish I'd thought of having my hair done like you did."

I went shopping too, looking for the right clothes to wear to play Mary Magdalene. Couldn't wear red. I tried on so many clothes. A black leather jacket. A flowing flowered dress, so cloaking. The harder I looked at myself in the dressing room mirror, the more I could see the swell of my nakedness beneath the dress, the plump arms and rolling thighs. I left outfits piled on the floors of dressing rooms till I found a knit skirt and a long, fitted cardigan. I wanted to look like someone who would not have to stoop to calculation to pull a man away from another woman, someone who couldn't help her power.

"Well, you look good too," I say. "Your scarf picks up the color of your eyes."

She shrugs. "I've been dieting. I haven't really gotten my figure back since I had Eli, and they say the TV cameras make you look fatter."

What I feel can't be so far from what she feels. She's excited too.

Anna Marie sorts a stack of curled photos from her old wallet. "I don't think this new wallet will hold all my pictures of Eli," she says. "You can help me pick out the best ones. Have you seen this one? We just had it done at the studio in the mall."

She'd be hurt if I didn't study the picture of her two-year-old grinning ferociously. "He looks like he's thinking about what he can do next to get in trouble."

"He doesn't have to think," Anna Marie says. "Trouble comes naturally to Eli. I had him in church with me last week, and I went up to Communion with him in my arms. When the priest gave me the host, my little guy pipes up, loud as you please, 'I want a cracker!' I mean, isn't that just the cutest thing?"

When Anna Marie talks to me about Eli, she is always asking me to answer the same questions, *isn't he cute, isn't he adorable,* with the utterly absorbed monotony of love. I'm only the honorary auntie. He *is* the cutest thing, with a head of curls and the deep, husky voice of a cartoon character. Once when I baby-sat for him, I had to distract him so Anna Marie could get ready to go out with Roger, and he wanted his mother. I tried to make a game out of blocking him from going to her in the bedroom, pretend we were playing tag, but he wouldn't be fooled. He struggled in my arms when I caught him. He bit me when I wouldn't let him go.

"Can't you tell me now what this show is all about?" Anna Marie says.

The show's producer sent us each a letter, strictly instructing us not to discuss our appearance with each other. "You know I'm not supposed to."

"Is it something to do with your mother?" Anna Marie says. "I thought maybe it was, because she's just passed on. But she didn't have any deep, dark secrets."

"Don't put me on the spot," I say.

"So then I'm thinking, what secret could there be that has to do with me?" Anna Marie taps a photo against her chin. "The only thing I can think of—this is silly—was maybe this is about Peter. It took me so long to figure out that he was a creep."

Shame floods my face at the sound of his name in her mouth. I'm bursting with the desire to tell her, but when we're alone, when there's nowhere else to look but at her, I can't open my mouth.

"You knew something about Peter, didn't you?" she says.

We ate in bed, afterward. I got up and fetched loaves of bread, fruit, blocks of cheese, the jam jar. We broke the food into crumbly bits. And Peter would scoop two fingers in the jam jar and smear jam on a chunk of bread and smash it into my mouth—*there, choke on it.* I never changed the sheets until the next time he came. Though I tried to brush them from the bed, the bread crumbs we left multiplied to infinity when I slept alone, sharp and hard as tiny crystals.

What do I know about Peter? He didn't even call me after he and Anna Marie broke up.

"Debbie, you didn't have to protect me," Anna Marie says. "I knew he was sleeping around. How can you not know with some part of yourself?"

She's the one who told me to go with him. They'd run out of ice at their party, and they'd been fighting that night, and if I didn't go with him to the liquor store, he'd ask another girl, the prettiest one he could find, just to rub salt in the wound. When we came back to the car with the ice, the bag split open all over the seat, and he and I were collecting the cold cubes in our hands, trying to stuff them back in the bag, and he started putting ice down my back, and I yanked him and pressed a handful under his collar to get back at him, and then we were kissing. I was so drunk. Sitting in his car in the dark parking lot, spitting on a Kleenex and trying to wipe smears of my lipstick from his face, I knew we'd find a time and a place to meet, as if it were an already accomplished fact. The way I've been knowing for years that Anna Marie has to find out.

"Don't worry," Anna Marie says. "I can laugh about it now. I've got Eli and Roger."

Whenever Anna Marie asks me to baby-sit for Eli, she acts as if she's bestowing a great favor, and she is. She tries to fix me up with guys too, inviting me over to watch football on Sundays with Roger and a bunch of his friends from work, coaching me on how to flirt. Who could bear this, forever and forever?

Our plane is met by a uniformed driver holding up a placard with our names on it, and Anna Marie and I are whisked off to the studio in a limousine. Anna Marie helps herself from the juice bar, slips off her shoes and sinks her feet in the thick carpet, devouring her taste of the star treatment. When we arrive at the studio, we are ushered to Makeup by a young woman named Candy who wears a headset. The smocked cosmetician works on Anna Marie first, and Anna Marie chatters giddily in the chair, says she feels like she's at a health spa. When it's my turn, I watch the glass as the cosmetician draws on me a face I would never wear out on the street. I'm pleased to be the person in the chair, relieved of all the anxiety about detail. When I'm snipping the fine ends of a client's hair, I know how hopeless it is to try and make such flimsy stuff truly even, would never finish if I did not look at the mirror instead of the few inches of hair pinched between my fingers.

Candy comes again to lead us each to separate rooms. Anna Marie asks her why we can't wait together, but Candy only smiles for answer. When I am alone in the waiting room—Candy calls it the green room—the awful sense of what I did visits like physical pain. This isn't the same thing as remembering. Only scattered pieces of what I did and felt come back, catching me unaware, with the force of a kick: the bitter smell of sex on my sheets after I'd been with Peter, a way he had of cupping my chin in his hand to turn my face to meet his, the word he used for what we did, *shtupping*. It happens so fast, hurts so swiftly, that there's no hope for using Molly's mental stop sign. One pain pulls another in its wake, and I find myself repeating the words of the confiteor: *Oh my God I am heartily sorry for having offended Thee.*

But these words are just reflex. I have in me only fragments of the grand slow music of my religion: *wherefore should I fear in the days of evil; behold the handmaid of the Lord; for the Lord spoke thus to me with a strong hand.* My mother knew her litanies by heart and made novenas for me. Even when she was dying, struggling with her illness and my father's fits of temper, she would tell me she was offering it up to God. "You go to God with your troubles, that's the answer." I'd want to ask her where it had gotten her—spending her life wishing and hoping and waiting on my father's whims, collecting her good china set at the supermarket, place setting by place setting. I'd want to tell her there was no one there waiting for the handoff.

I was able to fool myself only when I was alone with Peter. Then I could stand to think of Anna Marie, lash myself with the picture of him returning to her, jealousy drowning in the thrill and terror of betrayal, the sacrifice I'd made for him, and isn't that what saints do, torment themselves? It had to be love that made me kneel before him and press my mouth to the veins at his wrist, to the cushioned, unfeeling pad of his palm. And I wanted him to look down at me, worshiping him.

When I am called from the green room, I step onto the stage during a commercial break, sit down on a sofa on the dais. Vivian Woods stands before me, her back to the audience. Cameras are wheeled across the stage to set up for that moment when we'll be back on the air. The faces of the people in the audience remind me to cross my legs, sit like a lady. I feel giddy, powerful, imagining what will flicker on their faces when I tell my story.

Cued, Vivian announces me as her next guest in her authoritative, rat-a-tat voice. She reminds me of Oprah Winfrey, stocky, her hair tormented out of its natural kinks into a smooth shell, her eyes sharply outlined in pencil.

"You have a secret you want to share with us," Vivian says. "In a moment we're going to let your cousin listen in, but first I'd like you to tell us your story."

"Well, this happened about four years ago," I say. "I got involved with my cousin's boyfriend."

"You *slept* with your cousin's *boyfriend*?" Vivian is leading me, insinuating the shape and heft of my sin. "Wasn't he actually her fiancé at the time?"

"Yes."

"And what was the deal—was this some kind of one-night stand or some hot-and-heavy love affair?"

I don't know what to say, how to make anyone believe me.

"Now don't just sit there and shrug," Vivian says. "What was it—did you sleep with him once or a dozen times?"

"More than once."

"Five? Ten? Fifteen?"

"Maybe five or six times." Vivian looks disappointed. Smaller and smaller it shrinks, what I thought I had inside me raging to get out, to dimensions as exact as the set number of Hail Marys and Our Fathers the priest doles out in penance.

"Let's go back to the beginning," Vivian says. "How did this happen?"

"We went out to get ice for a party at his house, and we just started kissing in his car. They—he and my cousin were having trouble then. The relationship was kind of on the rocks."

"And you decided you'd give it a helpful push."

The audience laughs. I didn't really expect the Princess Di treatment. Peter pours cement for a living, and I give people bargain-basement haircuts. I feel the wrong kind of shame.

"So what happened then?" Vivian says. "Did you do it in the car while your cousin was waiting for you to come back with the ice?"

In the car when I wiped his face, Peter squeezed his eyes shut.

I bought a red kimono for those few nights he came to me. That flagrant, fearless color, just for him, just for that dark room.

"No," I say. "We went back to the party. Maybe a couple days later, he met me at my place. We met a couple times after that, and then we stopped."

"You and your cousin were close, right?"

"Yes."

"So what possessed you? What makes a woman betray her own family?"

Vivian's voice drops an octave on the word *betray*, that big word, but she's flogging it, trying to work up some interest.

"I thought I loved him," I say.

"And you never told your cousin?"

"No."

"Why tell her now, in front of a live television audience?"

"I guess I want to get it off my chest. Ask her to forgive me."

"You're saying you feel guilty, but you've got a smile on your face. Did you know you were smiling?"

I tuck my lower lip under my teeth. "I feel like I'm still lying to her every time I see her. Still doing it to her."

Vivian's face shifts readily to an expression of tenderness, so quickly and easily. "Well, we don't always get forgiveness. Sometimes we have to learn to forgive ourselves. We're going to see your cousin on the video screen now, and all I can promise you is the chance to ask."

I have to turn sideways on the couch to see Anna Marie's face on the big screen behind me, just a head and shoulders, eerily disembodied and enlarged.

"Anna Marie, this is about Peter," I say.

She nods as if she wants to help me.

I take a deep breath. "Remember back when you were breaking up with him?"

She nods again.

"Well, I was in love with him a little. You know, a crush. And then one thing led to another. You know. And I could never bring myself to tell you what happened."

I'm watching her face as avidly as the audience is: that worried, helping look gives way to shock, then to pain. I'm greedy for it, and God, yes, it's pleasure, watching like everyone else to see the damage, the visible proof that I've done something terrible.

Then she remembers she's on TV and looks down at her hands, fiercely reining in what shone so radiantly, so purely, from her face a moment ago. And I wanted to see it, what I had really done.

In her booth, Anna Marie can't see me, doesn't even know that I am looking at her. "I am so sorry," I say.

"Sure you are," Anna Marie says. "I know that."

To watch her blink so furiously brings tears to my eyes. This breach, this porousness, is forgiveness, isn't it?

"I just hated lying to you," I say. "It felt like—"

Vivian Woods interrupts me. "And can you find it in your heart to forgive her?" she asks Anna Marie. "Knowing what she's done and the burden of guilt she's been carrying?"

Watching Anna Marie's face on the video screen, I could be watching a movie. Her mouth puckers, and then she gives a quiet answer. Her words are as lost to me as the words I was going to say, words draped in velvet and shot through with gold threads. *Oh my God I am heartily sorry.*

Vivian Woods is already done with us, talking to the camera. "Don't go away, folks. After our next commercial break, Dr. Jean Dolan will talk about her new low-carbohydrate diet and show you how easy it can be to lose those extra pounds."

I wait for Anna Marie in the green room. Candy shows her in and asks when we'd like the limo to take us to the airport. Our flight's not scheduled for three more hours. "We could go now and probably get on an earlier flight," I say.

Anna Marie doesn't look at me.

"Would that be OK with you?" I ask her.

She shrugs. "Whatever you want."

Candy tells us she'll come back to fetch us when the limo arrives, and while we wait, we should help ourselves to coffee. "And don't hesitate to ask me for anything you need," she says, but her eyes are already glazed, her attention on whatever instructions are being sent over the headset she wears.

When Candy leaves, Anna Marie crosses the room and goes to the counter where the coffee service is arranged—a thermos, paper cups, packets of sugar, a half-and-half carton in a bucket of ice. She busies herself fixing a cup of coffee. I don't want a cup of coffee, but I go over there by her anyway. I pour a cup, fuss with the cream, a stirring stick. She doesn't move away.

Reaching for another packet of sugar, she knocks my hand, spilling my coffee.

"Oh, sorry," she says in her quiet voice.

She soaks up the spilled liquid with a wad of paper napkins. "Why'd you have to do this? Humiliate me in public. Wasn't it enough that you slept with him?"

"I needed your forgiveness."

"Oh, this is all about you, isn't it?"

She drags her hands over her face. "I called everyone I know and told them to watch. Roger stayed home from work with Eli so he could show him Mommy on TV. Remind me never to leave you alone with Roger again."

She looks at me, looks away. "Oh, gee, I'm sorry. That was below the belt."

"I never meant for it to happen," I say.

She covers her ears. "Please, please, please! Don't tell me about it. Do you think I want to add to the pictures in my mind?"

That man in the grocery store cupped my breast lightly enough not to compress it, as if it were an easily bruised fruit, as if he were merely tempted to take it and bite into it. As I would touch Peter, driven by the hunger of having him and not having him all at once. As I can search Anna Marie's face, hoping for one more glimpse of something pure and absolute.

I start to cry. "I didn't want to hurt you."

Anna Marie makes an irritated noise. "But you did."

I nod. If I open my mouth, excuses will come pouring out.

"Were you still seeing him when I came to you the night after we broke up? Were you humping him all that time you were telling me good riddance to bad rubbish, you'll see? Oh God, I feel kicked."

All I've done is to afflict her too with these pictures, with the helpless need to replay them over and over again. I reach for her.

"No! How dare you?" She steps back from me. "Were you jealous of me? Is that what this is about? Is that why you told me now—so you could take me down a peg? Is that what you wanted?"

What I wanted can't be read on her face, won't be held by any name she gives it. She can't even make herself look angry enough. Softness is natural to her, even when the cosmetician has painted it over so thoroughly.

Still, her voice is harsh. "I bet you told yourself you really loved him." She studies my face in a way that makes me feel she is looking through me to see something else. Then she makes a noise that might be triumph, might be dismay. "Oh my God, you did."

Now we've both been through it. Maybe now she can understand. What I want, just once, is to be truly beheld.

THE FLANNERY O'CONNOR
AWARD FOR SHORT FICTION

David Walton, *Evening Out*
Leigh Allison Wilson, *From the Bottom Up*
Sandra Thompson, *Close-Ups*
Susan Neville, *The Invention of Flight*
Mary Hood, *How Far She Went*
François Camoin, *Why Men Are Afraid of Women*
Molly Giles, *Rough Translations*
Daniel Curley, *Living with Snakes*
Peter Meinke, *The Piano Tuner*
Tony Ardizzone, *The Evening News*
Salvatore La Puma, *The Boys of Bensonhurst*
Melissa Pritchard, *Spirit Seizures*
Philip F. Deaver, *Silent Retreats*
Gail Galloway Adams, *The Purchase of Order*
Carole L. Glickfeld, *Useful Gifts*
Antonya Nelson, *The Expendables*
Nancy Zafris, *The People I Know*
Debra Monroe, *The Source of Trouble*
Robert H. Abel, *Ghost Traps*
T. M. McNally, *Low Flying Aircraft*
Alfred DePew, *The Melancholy of Departure*
Dennis Hathaway, *The Consequences of Desire*
Rita Ciresi, *Mother Rocket*
Dianne Nelson, *A Brief History of Male Nudes in America*
Christopher McIlroy, *All My Relations*
Alyce Miller, *The Nature of Longing*
Carol Lee Lorenzo, *Nervous Dancer*
C. M. Mayo, *Sky over El Nido*
Wendy Brenner, *Large Animals in Everyday Life*
Paul Rawlins, *No Lie Like Love*
Harvey Grossinger, *The Quarry*
Ha Jin, *Under the Red Flag*
Andy Plattner, *Winter Money*

Frank Soos, *Unified Field Theory*

Mary Clyde, *Survival Rates*

Hester Kaplan, *The Edge of Marriage*

Darrell Spencer, *CAUTION Men in Trees*

Robert Anderson, *Ice Age*

Bill Roorbach, *Big Bend*

Dana Johnson, *Break Any Woman Down*

Gina Ochsner, *The Necessary Grace to Fall*

Kellie Wells, *Compression Scars*

Eric Shade, *Eyesores*

Catherine Brady, *Curled in the Bed of Love*

Ed Allen, *Ate It Anyway*

Gary Fincke, *Sorry I Worried You*

Barbara Sutton, *The Send-Away Girl*

David Crouse, *Copy Cats*

Randy F. Nelson, *The Imaginary Lives of Mechanical Men*

Greg Downs, *Spit Baths*

Peter LaSalle, *Tell Borges If You See Him: Tales of Contemporary Somnambulism*

Anne Panning, *Super America*

Margot Singer, *The Pale of Settlement*

Andrew Porter, *The Theory of Light and Matter*

Peter Selgin, *Drowning Lessons*

Geoffrey Becker, *Black Elvis*

Lori Ostlund, *The Bigness of the World*

Linda LeGarde Grover, *The Dance Boots*

Jessica Treadway, *Please Come Back To Me*

Amina Gautier, *At-Risk*

Melinda Moustakis, *Bear Down, Bear North*

CPSIA information can be obtained at www.ICGtesting.com
Printed in the USA
LVOW040818290312

275030LV00003B/1/P